bellwether

D0792557

bellwether

connie willis

SPECTRA

bantam books

new york toronto london sydney auckland

BELLWETHER

A Bantam Spectra Book / April 1996

BOOK DESIGN BY CAROL MALCOLM RUSSO / SIGNET M DESIGN, INC.

Library of Congress Cataloging-in-Publication Data
Willis, Connie.
    Bellwether / Connie Willis.
       p.   cm.
    ISBN 0-553-37562-8
    I. Title.
PS3573.I45652B45   1996
813'.54—dc20   95-38615
                                      CIP

Published simultaneously in the United States and Canada

PRINTED IN THE UNITED STATES OF AMERICA

FFG   10 9 8 7 6 5 4 3 2 1

To John
From Abigail

"Yours—yours—yours—"

acknowledgment

Special thanks to the girls at Margie's Java Joint, who make the best caffè latte and conversation in the world, and without whom I wouldn't have made it through the last months of this novel!

1. beginning

Brothers, sisters, husbands, wives—
Followed the Piper for their lives.
From street to street he piped advancing,
And step by step they followed dancing.

robert browning

hula hoop (march 1958—june 1959)———The prototype for all merchandising fads and one whose phenomenal success has never been repeated. Originally a wooden exercise hoop used in Australian gym classes, the Hula Hoop was redesigned in gaudy plastic by Wham-O and sold for $1.98 to adults and kids alike. Nuns, Red Skelton, geishas, Jane Russell, and the Queen of Jordan rotated them on their hips, and lesser beings dislocated hips, sprained necks, and slipped disks. Russia and China banned them as "capitalist," a team of Belgian explorers took twenty of them along to the South Pole (to give the penguins?), and over fifty million were sold worldwide. Died out as quickly as it had spread.

It's almost impossible to pinpoint the beginning of a fad. By the time it starts to look like one, its origins are far in the past, and trying to trace them back is exponentially harder than, say, looking for the source of the Nile.

In the first place, there's probably more than one source, and in the second, you're dealing with human behavior. All Speke and Burton had to deal with were crocodiles, rapids, and the tsetse fly. In the third, we know something about how rivers work, like, they flow downhill. Fads seem to spring full-blown out of nowhere and for no good reason. Witness bungee-jumping. And Lava lamps.

Scientific discoveries are the same way. People like to think of science as rational and reasonable, following step by step from hypothesis to experiment to conclusion. Dr. Chin, last year's winner of the Niebnitz Grant, wrote, "The process of scientific discovery is the logical extension of observation by experimentation."

Nothing could be further from the truth. The process is exactly like any other human endeavor—messy, haphazard, misdirected, and heavily influenced by chance. Look at Alexander Fleming who discovered penicillin when a spore drifted in the window of his lab and contaminated one of his cultures.

Or Roentgen. He was working with a cathode-ray tube surrounded by sheets of black cardboard when he caught a glimpse of light from the other side of his lab. A sheet of paper coated with barium platinocyanide was fluorescing, even though it was shut off from the tube. Curious, he stuck his hand between the tube and the screen. And saw the shadow of the bones of his hand.

Look at Galvani, who was studying the nervous systems of frogs when he discovered electrical currents. Or Messier. He wasn't looking for galaxies when he discovered them. He was looking for comets. He only mapped them because he was trying to get rid of a nuisance.

None of which makes Dr. Chin any the less deserving of the Niebnitz Grant's million-dollar endowment. It isn't necessary to understand how something works to do it. Take driving. And starting fads. And falling in love.

What was I talking about? Oh, yes, how scientific discoveries come about. Usually the chain of events leading up to them, like that leading up to a fad, follows a course too convoluted and chaotic to follow. But I know exactly where one started and who started it.

It was in October. Monday the second. Nine o'clock in the morning. I was in the stats lab at HiTek, struggling with a box of clippings on hair-bobbing. I'm Sandra Foster, by the way, and I work in R&D at HiTek. I had spent all weekend going through yellowed newspapers and 1920s copies of *The Saturday Evening Post* and *The Delineator*, trudging upstream to the beginnings of the fad of hair-bobbing, looking for what had caused every woman in America to suddenly chop off her "crowning glory," despite social pressure, threatening sermons, and four thousand years of long hair.

I had clipped endless news items; highlighted references, magazine articles, and advertisements; dated them; and organized them into categories. Flip had stolen my stapler, I had run out of paper clips, and Desiderata hadn't been able to find any more, so I had had to settle for stacking them, in order, in the box, which I was now trying to maneuver into my lab.

The box was heavy and had been made by the same people who manufacture paper sacks at the supermarket, so when I'd dumped it just outside the lab so I could unlock the door, it had developed a major rip down one side. I was half-wrestling, half-dragging it over next to one of the lab tables so I could lift the stacks of clippings out when the whole side started to give way.

An avalanche of magazine pages and newspaper stories began to spill out through the side before I could get it pushed back in place, and I grabbed for them and the box as Flip opened the door and slouched in, looking disgusted. She was wearing black lipstick, a black halter, and a black leather micro-skirt and was carrying a box about the size of mine.

"I'm not *supposed* to have to deliver packages," she said. "You're *supposed* to pick them up in the mail room."

"I didn't know I had a package," I said, trying to hold the box together with one hand and reach a roll of duct tape in the middle of the lab table with the other. "Just set it down any-where."

She rolled her eyes. "You're *supposed* to get a notice saying you have a package."

Yes, well, and you were probably supposed to deliver it, I thought, which explains why I never got it. "Could you reach me that duct tape?" I said.

"Employees aren't supposed to ask interdepartmental as-sistants to run personal errands or make coffee," Flip said.

"Handing me a roll of tape is not a personal errand," I said.

Flip sighed. "I'm *supposed* to be delivering the interdepart-mental mail." She tossed her hair. She had shaved her head the week before but had left a long hank along the front and down one side expressly for flipping when she feels put-upon.

Flip is my punishment for having tried to get her prede-cessor, Desiderata, fired. Desiderata was mindless, clueless, and completely without initiative. She misdelivered the mail, wrote down messages wrong, and spent all her free time exam-ining her split ends. After two months and a wrong phone call that cost me a government grant, I went to Management and demanded she be fired and somebody, anybody else be hired, on the grounds that nobody could possibly be worse than De-siderata. I was wrong.

Management moved Desiderata to Supply (nobody ever gets fired at HiTek except scientists and even we don't get pink slips. Our projects just get canceled for lack of funding) and hired Flip, who has a nose ring, a tattoo of a snowy owl, and the habit of sighing and rolling her eyes when you ask her to do anything at all. I am afraid to get her fired. There is no telling who they might hire next.

Flip sighed loudly. "This package is really heavy."

"Then set it down," I said, stretching to reach the tape. It was just out of reach. I inched the hand holding the side of the box shut higher and leaned farther across the lab table. My fingertips just touched the tape.

"It's breakable," Flip said, coming over to me, and dropped the box. I grabbed to catch it with both hands. It thunked down on the table, the side gave way on *my* box, and the clippings poured out of the box and across the floor.

"Next time you're going to have to pick it up yourself," Flip said, walking on the clippings toward the door.

I shook the box, listening for broken sounds. There weren't any, and when I looked at the top, it didn't say FRAGILE anywhere. It said PERISHABLE. It also said DR. ALICIA TURNBULL.

"This isn't mine," I said, but Flip was already out the door. I waded through a sea of clippings and called to her. "This isn't my package. It's for Dr. Turnbull in Bio."

She sighed.

"You need to take this to Dr. Turnbull."

She rolled her eyes. "I have to deliver the rest of the interdepartmental mail *first*," she said, tossing her hank of hair. She slouched on down the hall, dropping two pieces of said departmental mail as she went.

"Make sure you come back and get it as soon as you're done with the mail," I shouted after her down the hall. "It's perishable," I shouted, and then, remembering that illiteracy is a hot trend these days and *perishable* is a four-syllable word, "That means it'll spoil."

Her shaved head didn't even turn, but one of the doors halfway down the hall opened, and Gina leaned out. "What did she do now?" she asked.

"Duct tape now qualifies as a personal errand," I said.

Gina came down the hall. "Did you get one of these?" she said, handing me a blue flyer. It was a meeting announcement. Wednesday. Cafeteria. All HiTek staff, including R&D. "Flip was supposed to deliver one to every office," she said.

"What's the meeting about?"

"Management went to another seminar," she said. "Which means a sensitivity exercise, a new acronym, and more paperwork for us. I think I'll call in sick. Brittany's birthday's in two weeks, and I need to get the party decorations. What's in these days in birthday parties? Circus? Wild West?"

"Power Rangers," I said. "Do you think they might reorganize the departments?" The last seminar Management had gone to, they'd created Flip's job as part of CRAM (Communications Reform Activation Management). Maybe this time they'd eliminate interdepartmental assistants, and I could go back to making my own copies, delivering my own messages, and fetching my own mail. All of which I was doing now.

"I *hate* the Power Rangers," Gina said. "Explain to me how they ever got to be so popular."

She went back to her lab, and I went back to work on my bobbed hair. It was easy to see how it had become popular. No long hair to put up with combs and pins and pompadour puffs, no having to wash it and wait a week for it to dry. The nurses who'd served in World War I had had to cut their hair off because of lice, and had liked the freedom and the lightness short hair gave them. And there were obvious advantages when it came to the other fads of the day: bicycling and lawn tennis.

So why hadn't it become a fad in 1918? Why had it waited another four years and then suddenly, for no apparent reason, hit so big that barber shops were swamped and hairpin companies went bankrupt overnight? In 1921, hair-bobbing was still unusual enough to make front-page news and get women fired. By 1925, it was so common every graduation picture and advertisement and magazine illustration showed short hair, and the only hats being sold were bell-shaped cloches, which were too snug to fit over long hair. What had happened in the interim? What was the trigger?

I spent the rest of the day re-sorting the clippings. You'd

think magazine pages from the 1920s would have turned yellowish and rough, but they hadn't. They'd slid like eels out onto the tile floor, fanning out across and under each other, mixing with the newspaper clippings and obliterating their categories. Some of the paper clips had even come off.

I did the re-sorting on the floor. One of the lab tables was full of clippings about pogs that Flip was supposed to have taken to be copied and hadn't, and the other one had all my jitterbug data on it. And neither one was big enough for the number of piles I needed, some of which overlapped: entire article devoted to hair-bobbing, reference within article devoted to flappers, pointed reference, casual reference, disapproving reference, humorous reference, shocked and horrified reference, illustration in advertisement, adoption by middle-aged women, adoption by children, adoption by the elderly, news items by date, news items by state, urban reference, rural reference, disparaging reference, reference indicating complete acceptance, first signs of waning of fad, fad declared over.

By 4:55 the floor of my whole lab was covered with piles and Flip still wasn't back. Stepping carefully among the piles, I went over and looked at the box again. Biology was clear on the other side of the complex, but there was nothing for it. The box said PERISHABLE, and even though irresponsibility is the hottest trend of the nineties, it hasn't worked its way through the whole society yet. I picked up the box and took it down to Dr. Turnbull.

It weighed a ton. By the time I'd maneuvered it down two flights and along four corridors, the reasons why irresponsibility had caught on had become very clear to me. At least I was getting to see a part of the building I ordinarily was never in. I wasn't even exactly sure where Bio was except that it was down on the ground floor. But I must be heading in the right direction. There was moisture in the air and a faint sound of zoo. I followed the sound down yet another staircase and into a long corridor. Dr. Turnbull's office was, of course, at the very end of it.

The door was shut. I shifted the box in my arms, knocked and waited. No answer. I shifted the box again, propping it against the wall with my hip, and tried the knob. The door was locked.

The last thing I wanted to do was lug this box all the way back up to my office and then try to find a refrigerator. I looked down the hall at the line of doors. They were all closed, and, presumably, locked, but there was a line of light under the middle one on the left.

I repositioned the box, which was getting heavier by the minute, lugged it down to the light, and knocked on the door. No answer, but when I tried the knob, the door opened onto a jungle of video cameras, computer equipment, opened boxes, and trailing wires.

"Hello," I said. "Anybody here?"

There was a muffled grunt, which I hoped wasn't from an inmate of the zoo. I glanced at the nameplate on the door. "Dr. O'Reilly?" I said.

"Yeah?" a man's voice from under what looked like a furnace said.

I walked around to the side of it and could see two brown corduroy legs sticking out from under it, surrounded by a litter of tools. "I've got a box here for Dr. Turnbull," I said to the legs. "She's not in her office. Could you take it for her?"

"Just set it down," the voice said impatiently.

I looked around for somewhere to set it that wasn't covered with video equipment and coils of chicken wire.

"Not on the equipment," the legs said sharply. "On the floor. *Carefully.*"

I pushed aside a rope and two modems and set the box

down. I squatted down next to the legs and said, "It's marked 'perishable.' You need to put it in the refrigerator."

"All *right*," he snapped. A freckled arm in a wrinkled white sleeve appeared, patting the floor around the base of the box.

There was a roll of duct tape lying just out of his reach. "Duct tape?" I said, putting it in his hand.

His hand closed around it and then just stayed there.

"You didn't want the duct tape?" I looked around to see what else he might have wanted. "Pliers? Phillips screwdriver?"

The legs and arm disappeared under the furnace and a head emerged from behind it. "Sorry," he said. His face was freckled, too, and he was wearing Coke-bottle-thick glasses. "I thought you were that mail person."

"Flip," I said. "No. She delivered the box to my office by mistake."

"Figures." He pulled himself out from under the furnace and stood up. "I really *am* sorry," he said, dusting himself off. "I don't usually act that rude to people who are trying to deliver things. It's just that Flip . . ."

"I know," I said, nodding sympathetically.

He pushed his hand through his sandy hair. "The last time she delivered a box to me she set it on top of one of the monitors, and it fell off and broke a video camera."

"That sounds like Flip," I said, but I wasn't really listening. I was looking at him.

When you spend as much time as I do analyzing fads and fashions, you get so you can spot them at first sight: eco-hippie, jogger, Wall Street M.B.A., urban terrorist. Dr. O'Reilly wasn't any of them. He was about my age and about my height. He was wearing a lab coat and corduroy pants that had been washed so often the wale was completely worn off on the knees. They'd shrunk, too, halfway up his ankles, and there was a pale line where they'd been let down.

The effect, especially with the Coke-bottle glasses, should have been science geek, but it wasn't. For one thing, there were the freckles. For another, he was wearing a pair of once-white canvas sneakers with holes in the toes and frayed seams. Science geeks wear black shoes and white socks. He wasn't even wearing a pocket protector, though he should have been. There were two splotches of ballpoint ink and a puddle of Magic Marker on the breast pocket of the lab coat, and one of the patch pockets was out at the bottom. And there was something else, something I couldn't put my finger on, that made it impossible for me to categorize him.

I squinted at him, trying to figure out exactly what it was, so long he looked at me curiously. "I took the box to Dr. Turnbull's office," I said hastily, "but she's gone home."

"She had a grant meeting today," he said. "She's very good at getting grants."

"The most important quality for a scientist these days," I said.

"Yeah," he said, smiling wryly. "Wish I had it."

"I'm Sandra Foster," I said, sticking out my hand. "Sociology."

He wiped his hand on his corduroys and shook my hand. "Bennett O'Reilly."

And that was odd, too. He was my age. His name should be Matt or Mike or, God forbid, Troy. Bennett.

I was staring again. I said, "And you're a biologist?"

"Chaos theory."

"Isn't that an oxymoron?" I said.

He grinned. "The way I did it, yes. Which is why my project lost its funding and I had to come to work for HiTek."

Maybe that accounted for the oddness, and corduroys and canvas sneakers were what chaos theorists were wearing these days. No, Dr. Applegate, over in Chem, had been in chaos, and he dressed like everybody else in R&D: flannel shirt, baseball cap, jeans, Nikes.

And nearly everybody at HiTek's working out of their field. Science has its fads and crazes, like anything else: string theory, eugenics, mesmerism. Chaos theory had been big for a couple of years, in spite of Utah and cold fusion, or maybe because of it, but both of them had been replaced by genetic engineering. If Dr. O'Reilly wanted grant money, he needed to give up chaos and build a better mouse.

He was stooping over the box. "I don't have a refrigerator. I'll have to set it outside on the porch." He picked it up, grunting a little. "Jeez, it's heavy. Flip probably delivered it to you on purpose so she wouldn't have to carry it all the way down here." He boosted it up with his corduroy knee. "Well, on behalf of Dr. Turnbull and all of Flip's other victims, thanks," he said, and headed into the tangle of equipment.

A clear exit line, and, speaking of grants, I still had half those hair-bobbing clippings to sort into piles before I went home. But I was still trying to put my finger on what it was that was so unusual about him. I followed him through the maze of stuff.

"Is Flip responsible for this?" I said, squeezing between two stacks of boxes.

"No," he said. "I'm setting up my new project." He stepped over a tangle of cords.

"Which is?" I brushed aside a hanging plastic net.

"Information diffusion." He opened a door and stepped outside onto a porch. "It should keep cold enough out here," he said, setting it down.

"Definitely," I said, hugging my arms against a chilly October wind. The porch faced a large, enclosed paddock, fenced in on all sides by high walls and overhead with wire netting. There was a gate at the back.

"It's used for large-animal experiments," Dr. O'Reilly said. "I'd hoped I'd have the monkeys by July so they could be outside, but the paperwork's taken longer than I expected."

"Monkeys?"

"The project's studying information diffusion patterns in a troop of macaques. You teach a new skill to one of the macaques and then document its spread through the troop. I'm working with the rate of utilitarian versus nonutilitarian skills. I teach one of the macaques a nonutilitarian skill with a low ability threshold and multiple skill levels—"

"Like the Hula Hoop," I said.

He set the box down just outside the door and stood up. "The Hula Hoop?"

"The Hula Hoop, miniature golf, the twist. All fads have a low ability threshold. That's why you never see speed chess becoming a fad. Or fencing."

He pushed his Coke-bottle glasses up on his nose.

"I'm working on a project on fads. What causes them and where they come from," I said.

"Where do they come from?"

"I have no idea. And if I don't get back to work, I never will." I stuck out my hand again. "Nice to have met you, Dr. O'Reilly." I started back through the maze.

He followed me, saying thoughtfully, "I never thought of teaching them to do a Hula Hoop."

I was going to say I didn't think there'd be room in here, but it was almost six, and I at least had to get my piles up off the floor and into file folders before I went home.

I told Dr. O'Reilly goodbye and went back up to Sociology. Flip was standing in the hall, her hands on the hips of her leather skirt.

"I *came* back and you'd *left*," she said, making it sound like I'd left her sinking in quicksand.

"I was down in Bio," I said.

"I had to come all the way back from Personnel," she said, tossing her hair. "You *said* to come back."

"I gave up on you and delivered the package myself," I said, waiting for her to protest and say delivering the mail was her job. I should have known better. That would have meant admitting she was actually responsible for something.

"I looked all over your office for it," she said virtuously. "While I was waiting for you, I picked up all that stuff you left on the floor and threw it in the trash."

the old curiosity shop (1840—41)

Book fad caused by serialization of Dickens's story about a little girl and her hapless grandfather, who are thrown out of their shop and forced to wander through England. Interest in the book was so great that people in America thronged the pier waiting for the ship from England to bring the next installment and, unable to wait for the ship to dock, shouted to the passengers aboard, "Did Little Nell die?" She did, and her death reduced readers of all ages, sexes, and degrees of toughness to agonies of grief. Cowboys and miners in the West sobbed openly over the last pages and an Irish member of Parliament threw the book out of a train and burst into tears.

The source of the Thames doesn't look like it. It looks like a pasture, and not even a soggy pasture. Not a single water plant grows there. If it weren't for an old well, filled up with stones, it would be impossible to even locate the spot. Cows, not being interested in stones, wander lazily across and around the source, munching buttercups and Queen Anne's lace, unaware that anything significant is beginning beneath their feet.

Science is even less obvious. It starts with an apple falling, a teakettle boiling. Alex Fleming, taking a last glance around his lab as he left for a long weekend, wouldn't have seen anything significant in the window left half open, in the sooty air from Paddington Station drifting in. Getting ready to gather up his notes, to tell his assistant to leave everything alone, to lock the door, he wouldn't have noticed that one of the petri dishes' lids had slid a fraction of an inch to the side. His mind would have already been on his vacation, on the errands he had to run, on going home.

So was mine. The only thing I was aware of was that Flip had thoughtfully crumpled each clipping into a wad before stuffing them into the trash can, and that there was no way I could get them all smoothed out tonight, and, as a result, I was not only oblivious to the first event in a chain of events that was going to lead to a scientific discovery, but I was about to miss the second one, too. And the third.

I set the trash can on the lab table on top of my jitterbug research, sealed the top with duct tape, stuck on a sign that said "*Do not* touch. This means you, Flip," and went out to my car. Halfway out of the parking lot I thought about Flip's ability to read, turned around, and went back to my office to get the trash can.

The phone was ringing when I opened the door. "Howdy," Billy Ray said when I picked it up. "Guess where I am."

"In Wyoming?" I said. Billy Ray was a rancher from Laramie I'd gone out with a while back when I was researching line dancing.

"In Montana," he said. "Halfway between Lodge Grass and Billings." Which meant he was calling me on his cellular phone. "I'm on my way to look at some Targhees," he said. "They're the hottest thing going."

I assumed they were also cows. During my line dancing phase, the hottest thing going had been Aberdeen Longhorns. Billy Ray is a very nice guy and a walking compendium of country-western fads. Two birds with one stone.

"I'm going to be in Denver this Saturday," he said through the stutter that meant his cellular phone was starting to get out of range. "For a seminar on computerized ranching."

I wondered idly what its acronym would be. Computerized Operational Wrangling?

"So I wondered if we could grab us some dinner. There's a new prairie place in Boulder."

And prairie was the latest thing in cuisine. "Sorry," I said, looking at the trash can on my lab table. "I've had a setback. I'm going to have to work this weekend."

"You should just feed everything onto your computer and let it do the work. I've got my whole ranch on my PC."

"I know," I said, wishing it were that simple.

"You need to get yourself one of those text scanners," Billy Ray said, the hum becoming more insistent. "That way you don't even have to type it in."

I wondered if a text scanner could read crumpled.

The hum was becoming a crackle. "Well, maybe next time," he sort of said, and passed into cellular oblivion.

I put down my noncellular phone and picked up the trash can. Under it, half buried in my jitterbug research, were the library books I should have taken back two days ago. I piled them on top of the stretched duct tape, which held, and carried them and the trash can out to the car and drove to the library.

Since I spend my working days studying trends, many of which are downright disgusting, I feel it's my duty after work to encourage the trends I'd like to see catch on, like signaling before you change lanes, and chocolate cheesecake. And reading.

Also, libraries are great places to observe trends in bestsellers, and library management. And librarian attire.

"What's on the reserve list this week, Lorraine?" I asked

the librarian at the desk. She was wearing a black-and-white-mottled sweatshirt with the logo UDDERLY FANTASTIC on it, and a pair of black-and-white Holstein cow earrings.

"*Led On by Fate*," she said. "Still. The reserve list's a foot long. You are"—she counted down her computer screen—"fifth in line. You were sixth, but Mrs. Roxbury canceled."

"Really?" I said, interested. Book fads don't usually die out until the sequel comes out, at which point the readers realize they've been had. Witness *Oliver's Story* and *Slow Waltz at Cedar Bend*. Which is why the *Gone with the Wind* trend managed to last nearly six years, resulting in thousands of unhappy little boys having to live down the name of Rhett, or even worse, Ashley. If Margaret Mitchell'd come out with *Slow Waltz at Tara Bend* it would have been all over. Which reminded me, I should check to see if there'd been any drop-off in *Gone with the Wind*'s popularity since the publication of *Scarlett*.

"Don't get your hopes up about *Fate*," Lorraine said. "Mrs. Roxbury only canceled because she said she couldn't bear to wait for it and bought her own copy." She shook her head, and her cows swung back and forth. "What *do* people see in it?"

Yes, well, and what did they see in *Little Lord Fauntleroy* back in the 1890s, Frances Hodgson Burnett's sickly sweet tale of a little boy with long curls who inherited an English castle? Whatever it was, it made the novel into a best-seller and then a hit play and a movie starring Mary Pickford (she already had the long curls), started a style of velvet suits, and became the bane of an earlier generation of little boys whose mothers inflicted lace collars, curlers, and the name Cedric on them and who would have been delighted to have only been named Ashley.

"What else is on the reserve list?"

"The new John Grisham, the new Stephen King, *Angels*

from Above, Brushed by an Angel's Wing, Heavenly Encounters of the Third Kind, Angels Beside You, Angels, Angels Everywhere, Putting Your Guardian Angel to Work for You, and *Angels in the Boardroom.*"

None of those counted. The Grisham and the Stephen King were only best-sellers, and the angel fad had been around for over a year.

"Do you want me to put you on the list for any of those?" Lorraine asked. "*Angels in the Boardroom* is great."

"No, thanks," I said. "Nothing new, huh?"

She frowned. "I thought there was something . . ." She checked her computer screen. "The novelization of *Little Women,*" she said, "but that wasn't it."

I thanked her and went over to the stacks. I picked out F. Scott Fitzgerald's "Bernice Bobs Her Hair" and a couple of mysteries, which always have simple, solvable problems like "How did the murderer get into the locked room?" instead of hard ones like "What causes trends?" and "What did I do to deserve Flip?" and then went over to the eight hundreds.

One of the nastier trends in library management in recent years is the notion that libraries should be "responsive to their patrons." This means having dozens of copies of *The Bridges of Madison County* and Danielle Steel, and a consequent shortage of shelf space, to cope with which librarians have taken to purging books that haven't been checked out lately.

"Why are you throwing out Dickens?" I'd asked Lorraine last year at the library book sale, brandishing a copy of *Bleak House* at her. "You can't throw out Dickens."

"Nobody checked it out," she'd said. "If no one checks a book out for a year, it gets taken off the shelves." She had been wearing a sweatshirt that said A TEDDY BEAR IS FOREVER, and a pair of plush teddy bear earrings. "Obviously nobody read it."

"And nobody ever will because it won't be there for them to check out," I'd said. "*Bleak House* is a wonderful book."

"Then this is your chance to buy it," she'd said.

Well, and this was a trend like any other, and as a sociologist I should note it with interest and try to determine its origins. I didn't. Instead, I started checking out books. All my favorites, which I'd never checked out because I had copies at home, and all the classics, and everything with an old cloth binding that somebody might want to read someday when the current trends of sentimentality and schlock are over.

Today I checked out *The Wrong Box*, in honor of the day's events, and since I'd first seen Dr. O'Reilly with his legs sticking out from under a large object, *The Wizard of Oz*, and then went over to the Bs to look for Bennett. *The Old Wives' Tale* wasn't there (it had probably ended up in the book sale already), but right next to Beckett was Butler's *The Way of All Flesh*, which meant *The Old Wives' Tale* might just be misshelved.

I started down the shelves, looking for something chubby, clothbound, and untouched. Borges; *Wuthering Heights*, which I had already checked out this year; Rupert Brooke. And Robert Browning. *The Complete Works*. It wasn't Arnold Bennett, but it was both clothbound and fat, and it still had an old-fashioned pocket and checkout card in it. I grabbed it and the Borges and took them to the checkout desk.

"I remembered what else was on the reserve list," Lorraine said. "New book. *Guide to the Fairies*."

"What is it, a children's book?"

"No." She took it off the reserve shelf. "It's about the presence of fairies in our daily lives."

She handed it to me. It had a picture of a fairy peeking out from behind a computer on the cover, and it fit one of the criteria for a book fad: It was only 80 pages long. *The Bridges of Madison County* was 192 pages, *Jonathan Livingston Seagull* was

93, and *Goodbye, Mr. Chips*, a huge fad back in 1934, was only 84.

It was also drivel. The chapter titles were "How to Get in Touch with Your Inner Fairy," "How Fairies Can Help Us Get Ahead in the Corporate World," and "Why You Shouldn't Pay Attention to Unbelievers."

"You'd better put me on the list," I said. I handed her the Browning.

"This hasn't been checked out in nearly a year," she said.

"Really?" I said. "Well, it is now." And took my Borges, Browning, and Baum and went to get some dinner at the Earth Mother.

poulaines (1350—1480) — Soft leather or cloth shoes with elongated points. Originating in Poland (hence *poulaine;* the English called them *crackowes* after Cracow), or more logically brought back from the Middle East by Crusaders, they became the craze at all the European courts. The pointed toes became more elaborate, stuffed with moss and shaped into lions' claws or eagles' beaks, and progressively longer, to the point that it was impossible to walk without tripping over them and completely impossible to kneel, and gold and silver chains had to be attached to the knees to hold up the ends. Translated into armor, the poulaine fad became downright dangerous: Austrian knights at the battle of Sempach in 1386 were riveted to the spot by their elongated iron shoes and were forced to strike off the points with their swords or be caught flat-footed, so to speak. Supplanted by the square-toed, ankle-strapped duck's-bill shoe, which promptly became ridiculously wide.

The Earth Mother has okay food and iced tea so good I order it all year round. Plus, it's a great place to study fads. Not only is its menu trendy (currently free-range vegetarian), but so are its waiters. Also, there's a stand outside with all the alternative newspapers.

I gathered them up and went inside. The door and entry-way were jammed with people waiting to get in. Their iced tea must be becoming a trend. I presented myself to the waitress, who had a prison-style haircut, jogging shorts, and Tevas.

That's another trend, waitresses dressed to look as little as possible like waitresses, probably so you can't find them when you want your check. "Name and number in your party?" the waitress said. She was holding a tablet with at least twenty names.

"One, Foster," I said. "I'll take smoking or nonsmoking, whichever's quicker."

She looked outraged. "We don't *have* a smoking section," she said. "Don't you know what smoking can do to you?"

Usually get you seated quicker, I thought, but since she looked ready to cross out my name, I said, "*I* don't smoke. I was just willing to sit with people who do."

"Secondhand smoke is just as deadly," she said, and put an *X* next to my name that probably meant I would be seated right after hell froze over. "I'll call you," she said, rolling her eyes, and I certainly hoped *that* wasn't a trend.

I sat down on the bench next to the door and started through the papers. They were full of animal rights articles and tattoo removal ads. I turned to the personals. The personals aren't a fad. They were, in the late eighties, and then, like a lot of fads, instead of dying out, they settled into a small but permanent niche in society.

That happens to lots of fads: CBs were so popular for a few months that "Breaker, breaker" became a catchphrase and everyone had handles like "Red Hot Mama," and then went back to being used by truckers and speeding motorists. Bi-cycles, Monopoly, crossword puzzles, all were crazes that have settled into the mainstream. The personals took up residence in the alternative newspapers.

There can be trends within trends, though, and the personals go through fads of their own. Unusual varieties of sex was big for a while. Now it's outdoor activities.

The waitress, looking vastly disapproving, said, "Foster party of one," and led me to a table right in front of the kitchen. "We banned smoking two *years* ago," she said, and slapped down a menu.

I picked it up, glanced at it to see if they still had the sprouts and sun-dried tomatoes croissant, and settled down to the personals again. Jogging was out, and mountain biking and kayaking were in. And angels. One of the ads was headed HEAVENLY MESSENGER and another one said "Are your angels telling you to call me? Mine told me to write this ad," which I found unlikely.

Soul work was also in, and spirituality, and slashes. "S/ DWF wanted," and "Into Eastern/Native American/personal growth," and "Seeking fun/possible life partner." Well, aren't we all?

A waiter appeared, also in jogging shorts, Tevas, and snit. He had apparently seen the *X*. I said, before he could lecture me on the dangers of nicotine, "I'll have the sprouts croissant and iced tea."

"We don't have that anymore."

"Sprouts?"

"Tea." He flipped the menu open and pointed to the right-hand page. "Our beverages are right here."

They certainly were. The entire page was devoted to them: espresso, cappuccino, caffè latte, caffè mocha, caffè cacao. But no tea. "I liked your iced tea," I said.

"No one drinks tea anymore," he said.

Because you took it off the menu, I thought, wondering if they'd used the same principle as the library, and I should have come here more often, or ordered more than one when I did come, and saved it from the ax. Also feeling guilty because I'd apparently missed the start of a trend, or at least a new stage in one.

The espresso trend's actually been around for several years, mostly on the West Coast and in Seattle, where it started. A lot of fads have come out of Seattle recently—garage bands, the grunge look, caffè latte. Before that, fads usually started in L.A., and before that, New York. Lately, Boulder's shown signs of becoming the next trend center, but the spread of espresso to Boulder probably has more to do with bottom lines than the scientific laws of fads, but I still wished I'd been around to watch it happen and see if I could spot the trigger.

"I'll have a caffè latte," I said.

"Single or double?"

"Double."

"Tall or short?"

"Tall."

"Chocolate or cinnamon on top?"

"Chocolate."

"Semisweet or dark?"

I'd been wrong when I told Dr. O'Reilly all fads had to have a low ability threshold.

After several more exchanges, concerning whether I wanted cubed sugar versus brown and nonfat versus two percent, he left, and I went back to the personals.

Honesty was out, as usual. The men were all "tall, handsome, and financially secure," and the women were all "gorgeous, slender, and sensitive." The G/Bs were all "attractive, sophisticated, and caring." Everyone had a "terrific sense of humor," which I also found unlikely. All of them were seeking sensitive, intelligent, ecological, romantic, articulate NSs.

NS. What was NS? Nordic skiing? Native American Shamanism? Natural sex? No sex? And here was NSO. No sexual orgasms? I flipped back to the translation guide. Of course. Nonsmoker only.

The buxom, handsome, caring people who place these things seem frequently to have confused the personals with the L. L. Bean catalog: I'd like Item D2481 in passion red. Size, small. And they frequently specify color, shape, and no pets. But the number of nonsmokings seemed to have radically increased since the last time I'd done a count. I got a red pen out of my purse and started to circle them.

By the time my sandwich and complex latte had arrived, the page was covered in red. I ate my sandwich and sipped my latte and circled.

The nonsmoking trend started way back in the late seventies, and so far it had followed the typical pattern for aversion trends, but I wondered if it was starting to reach another, more volatile level. "Any race, religion, political party, sexual preference okay," one of the ads read. "NO SMOKERS." In caps.

And "Must be adventurous, daring, nonsmoking risktaker" and "Me: Successful but tired of being alone. You: Compassionate, caring, nonsmoking, childless." And my favorite: "Desperately seeking someone who marches to the beat of a different drummer, flouts convention, doesn't care what's in or out. Smokers need not apply."

Someone was standing over me. The waiter, probably, wanting to give me a nicotine patch. I looked up.

"I didn't know *you* came here," Flip said, rolling her eyes.

"I didn't know you came here either," I said. And now that I do I never will again, I thought. Especially since they don't serve iced tea anymore.

"The personals, huh?" she said, craning around to look at what I'd marked. "They're okay, I guess, if you're desperate."

I am, I thought, wondering wildly if she'd stopped on the way in to empty the trash and had I locked the car?

"*I* don't need artificial aids. *I* have Brine," she said, pointing at a guy with a shaved head, bovver boots, and studs in his nose, eyebrows, and lower lip, but I wasn't looking at him. I was looking at her extended arm, which had three wide gray armlets around it at wrist, mid-forearm, and just below the elbow. Duct tape.

Which explained her remark about it being a personal errand this afternoon. If this is the latest fad, I thought, I quit. "I have to go," I said, scooping up my newspapers and purse, and looking frantically around for my waiter, who I couldn't find since he was dressed like everybody else. I put down a twenty and practically ran for the exit.

"She doesn't appreciate me at all," I heard Flip telling Brine as I fled. "She could at least have thanked me for cleaning up her office."

I *had* locked my car, and, driving home, I began to feel almost cheerful about the duct tape armbands. Flip would, after all, have to take them off. I also thought about Brine and about Billy Ray, who wears a Stetson and boot-cut jeans and a pager, and about what an accomplishment Dr. O'Reilly's unstylishness really was.

Almost everything is in style for men these days: bomber jackets, bicycle pants, dashikis, *GQ* suits, jeans that are too big, tank shirts that are too small, deck shoes, hiking boots, Birkenstocks. And now with the addition of grunge's faded flannel shirts and thermal underwear, it's hard to find anything that looks bad enough to not be in style. But Dr. O'Reilly had managed it.

His hair was too long and his pants were too short, but it was more than that. One of the garage bands has a drummer who wears pedal pushers and braids onstage, and he looks like the ultimate in trendiness. And it wasn't his glasses. Look at Elton John. Look at Buddy Holly.

It was something else, something that had been nagging at

me all evening. Maybe I should go back down to Bio and ask him if I could study him. Maybe if I followed him around while he taught his monkeys to Hula Hoop or whatever it was he was going to do, I could figure out how he managed to be trend-free. And by studying a nontrend, get some clue to its opposite. Or maybe I should go home, iron my clippings, and try to figure out what caused two million women to suddenly pick up their scissors in unison and whack off their Little Lord Fauntleroy curls.

I didn't do either one. Instead, I went home and read Browning. I read "The Pied Piper," a poem which, oddly enough, was about fads, and started *Pippa Passes*, a long poem about an Italian factory girl in Asolo who only got one day a year off (clearly she worked for the Italian branch of HiTek) and who spent it wandering past windows singing, among other things, "The lark's on the wing;/The snail's on the thorn," and inspiring everybody who heard her.

I wished she'd show up outside my window and inspire me, but it didn't seem likely. Inspiration was going to have to come the way it usually did in science, uncrumpling all those clippings and feeding the data into the computer. By experimenting and failing and trying again.

I was wrong. Inspiration had already happened. I just didn't know it yet.

quality circles (1980—85)———Business fad inspired by successful Japanese corporate practices. A committee of employees from all areas of the company would meet once a month, usually after work, to share experiences, communicate ideas, and make suggestions as to ways the corporation could be better run. Died out when it became apparent that none of those suggestions were being taken. Replaced by QIS, MBO, JIT, and hot groups.

Wednesday we had the all-staff meeting. I was nearly late to it. I'd been down in Supply, trying to wrestle a box of paper clips out of Desiderata, who didn't know where (or what) they were, and, as a result, every table in the cafeteria was filled when I got there.

Gina waved to me from across the room and pointed at an empty chair next to her, and I slid into it just as Management said, "We at HiTek never stop striving for excellence."

"What's going on?" I whispered to Gina.

"Management is proving beyond a shadow of a doubt they don't have enough to do," she murmured back. "So they've invented a new acronym. They're working up to it right now."

". . . principle of our exciting new management program is Initiative." He printed a large capital *I* on a flipchart with a

Magic Marker. "Initiative is the cornerstone of a good company."

I looked around the room, trying to spot Dr. O'Reilly. Flip was slouched against the back wall, her arms swathed in duct tape, looking sullen.

"The cornerstone of Initiative is Resources," Management said. He printed an *R* in front of the *I*. "And what is HiTek's most valuable resource? You!"

I finally spotted Dr. O'Reilly standing near the trays and the silverware with his hands in his pockets. He looked a little more presentable today, but not much. He'd put a brown polyester blazer on that wasn't the same brown as his corduroy pants and a brown-and-white-checked shirt that didn't match either one.

"Resources and Initiative are worthless unless they're guided," Management said, sticking a *G* in front of the *R* and *I*. "Guided Resource Initiative Management," he said triumphantly, pointing to each letter in turn. "GRIM."

"Truer words," Gina muttered.

"The cornerstone of GRIM is Staff Input." Management wrote *SI* on the flip chart. "I want you to divide into brainstorming groups and list five objectives." He wrote a large *5* on the flipchart.

I looked over at Dr. O'Reilly, still standing by the silverware, wondering if I should invite him to join our brainstorming group, but Gina'd already grabbed Sarah from Chemistry and a woman from Personnel named Elaine who was wearing a sweatband and bicycle pants.

"*Five* objectives," Management said, and Elaine immediately got out a notebook and numbered a page from one to five, "for enhancing the work environment at HiTek."

"Fire Flip," I said.

"Do you know what she did to me the other day?" Sarah said. "She filed all my lab charts under *L* for lab."

"Should I write that down?" Elaine said.

"No," Gina said, "but I want you *all* to write this down. Brittany's birthday is on the eighteenth and you're all invited. Two o'clock. Presents, cake, and *no* Power Rangers. I put my foot down. You can have any kind of party you want, I told Brittany, but *not* Power Rangers."

Dr. O'Reilly had finally sat down at a table in the middle of the room and had taken off his jacket. It wasn't an improvement. All it meant was that you could see his tie, which was seriously out of style.

"Have you ever *seen* the Power Rangers?" Gina was saying.

"I can't come," Sarah said. "I'm running in a ten-K race with Paul Ottermeyer."

"In Safety? I thought you were going with Ted," Gina said.

"Ted has intimacy issues," Sarah said. "And until he learns to deal with them, there's no point in our trying to have a committed relationship."

"So you're settling for a ten-K race?" Gina said.

"You should try stair-walking," Elaine from Personnel said. "It gives you a much better full-body workout than running."

I leaned my chin on my hand and considered Dr. O'Reilly's tie. Ties are a lot like the rest of men's clothes. Almost everything's in. That wasn't true until recently. Each era had its own fashion in ties. Striped cravats were in in the 1860s and lavender ties in the 1890s. Bow ties were big in the twenties, hand-painted hula dancers in the forties, neon daisies in the sixties, and anything that wasn't in was out. But now all of the above are in, along with bolos, bandannas, and the ever-popular no tie at all. Bennett's tie wasn't any of those—it was just ugly.

"What are you looking at?" Gina asked.

"Dr. O'Reilly," I said, wondering if he was old enough to have bought the tie new.

"The geek down in Bio?" Elaine said, craning her neck.

"Bad tie," Gina said.

"And those glasses," Sarah said. "They're so thick you can't even tell what color his eyes are!"

"Gray," I said, but Elaine and Sarah had gone back to discussing stair-walking.

"The best stairs are up on campus," Elaine said. "The engineering building. Sixty-eight steps, but it's gotten pretty crowded. So I usually do the ones over on Clover."

"Ted lives on Iris," Sarah said. "He's got to acknowledge his male warrior spirit, or he'll never be able to embrace his female side."

"All right, fellow workers," Management said. "Do you have your five objectives? Flip, would you collect them?"

Elaine looked stricken. Gina snatched the list from her and wrote rapidly:

1. Optimize potential.
2. Facilitate empowerment.
3. Implement visioning.
4. Strategize priorities.
5. Augment core structures.

"How did you do that?" I said admiringly.

"Those are the five things I always write down," she said and handed the list to Flip as she slouched past.

"Before we go any further," Management said, "I want you all to stand up."

"Bathroom break," Gina murmured.

"We're going to do a sensitivity exercise," Management said. "Everybody find a partner."

I turned. Sarah and Elaine had already claimed each

other, and Gina was nowhere to be seen. I hesitated, wondering if I could make it all the way over to Dr. O'Reilly in time, and saw a woman in a chic haircut and a red power suit moving purposefully through the crowd to me.

"I'm Dr. Alicia Turnbull," she said.

"Oh, right," I said, smiling. "Did you get your box okay?"

"Everybody got a partner?" Management boomed. "Now, face each other and raise both hands, palms outward."

We did. "You're all under arrest," I joked.

Dr. Turnbull raised an eyebrow.

"Okay, fellow workers," Management said, "now place your palms flat against the palms of your partner's hands."

Silliness has always been a dominant trend in America, but it has only recently invaded the workplace, although it has its origins in the efficiency experts of the twenties. Frank and Lillian Gilbreth, the founders of the *Cheaper by the Dozen* clan, who clearly did *not* spend all their time in the factory (twelve children, count 'em, twelve), popularized the ideas of motion study, psychology in the workplace, and the outside expert, and American business has been in decline ever since.

"Now, look *deep* in your partner's eyes," Management said, "and tell him or her three things you like about him or her. Okay. One."

"Where *do* they come up with this stuff?" I said, looking deep in Dr. Turnbull's eyes.

"Studies have shown sensitivity training significantly improves corporate workplace relations," she said frostily.

"Fine," I said. "You go first."

"That package clearly said 'perishable' on it," she said, pressing her palms against mine. "You should have delivered it to me immediately."

"You weren't there."

"Then you should have found out where I was."

"Two," Management said.

"That package contained valuable cultures. They could have spoiled."

She seemed to have lost sight of an important point here. "*Flip* was the one who was supposed to have delivered it to you."

"Then what was it doing in your office?"

"Three," Management said.

"Next time I'd appreciate it if you'd leave a message on my e-mail," she said. "Well? Aren't you going to tell me three things you like about me? It's your turn."

I like it that you work in Bio and that it's clear on the other end of the complex, I thought. "I like your suit," I said, "even though shoulder pads are terribly passé. And so is red. Too threatening. Feminine is what's in."

"Don't you feel better about yourself?" Management said, beaming. "Don't you feel closer to your fellow worker?"

Too close, in fact. I beat a hasty retreat back to my table and Gina. "Where did you go?" I demanded.

"To the bathroom," she said. "Meeting Survival Rule Number One. Always be out going to the bathroom during sensitivity exercises."

"Before we go any further," Management said, and I braced myself to make a break for the bathroom in case of another sensitivity exercise, but Management was moving right along to the increased paperwork portion of our program, which turned out to be procurement forms.

"We've had some complaints about Supply," Management said, "so we've instituted a new policy that will increase efficiency in that department. Instead of the old departmental supply forms, you'll use a new interdepartmental form. We've also restructured the funding allocation procedure. One of the most revolutionary aspects of GRIM is the way it streamlines funding. All applications for project funding will be handled by a central Allocations Review Committee, including projects which were previously approved. All forms are due Monday the twenty-third. All applications must be filed on the new simplified funding allocation application forms."

Which, if the stack of papers Flip was holding in her duct-taped arms as she passed among the crowd was any indication, were longer than the old funding application forms, and *they* were thirty-two pages.

"While the interdepartmental assistant's distributing the forms, I want to hear your input. What else can we do to make HiTek a better place?"

Eliminate staff meetings, I thought, but didn't say it. I may not be as well versed as Gina is in Meeting Survival, but I do know enough not to raise my hand. All it does is get you put on a committee.

Apparently everybody else knew it, too.

"Staff Input is the cornerstone of HiTek," he said.

Still nothing.

"*Anybody?*" Management said, looking GRIM. He brightened. "Ah, at last, someone who's not afraid to stand out in a crowd."

Everybody turned to look.

It was Flip. "The interdepartmental assistant has way too many duties," she said, flipping her hank of hair.

"You see," Management said, pointing at her. "That's the kind of problem-solving attitude that GRIM is all about. What solution do you suggest?"

"A different job title," Flip said. "And an assistant."

I looked across the room at Dr. O'Reilly. He had his head in his hands.

"Okay. Other ideas?"

Forty hands shot up. I looked at the waving hands and thought about the Pied Piper and his rats. And about hair-bobbing. Most hair fads are a clear case of follow-the-Piper. Bo Derek, Dorothy Hamill, Jackie Kennedy, had all started hairstyle fads, and they were by no means the first. Madame de Pompadour had been responsible for those enormous powdered wigs with sailing ships and famous artillery battles in them, and Veronica Lake for millions of American women being unable to see out of one eye.

So it was logical that hair-bobbing had been started by somebody, only who? Isadora Duncan had bobbed her hair in the early 1900s, and several suffragettes had bobbed theirs (and put on men's clothes) long before that, but neither had attracted any followers to speak of.

The suffragettes were obviously ahead of their time (and rather fearsomely formidable). Isadora, who leaped around the stage in skimpy chiffon tunics and bare feet, was too weird.

The obvious person was the ballroom dancer Irene Castle. She and her husband, Vernon (more miserable little boys), had set several dancing trends: the one-step, the hesitation waltz, the tango, the turkey trot, and, of course, the Castle Walk.

Irene was pretty, and almost everything she wore had become a fad, from white satin shoes to little Dutch caps. In 1913, at the height of their popularity, she'd had her hair cut short while she was in the hospital after an appendectomy, and she'd kept it short after she got better and had worn it with a wide band that clearly foreshadowed the flappers.

She was a known fashion-setter, and she'd definitely had followers. But if she was the source, why had it taken so long to catch on? When Bo Derek's corn-rowed hair hit movie screens in 1979, it was only a week before corn-rowed women started showing up everywhere. If Irene was the source, why hadn't hair-bobbing become a fad in 1913? Why had it waited for nine years and a world war to become a fad?

Maybe the movies were the key. No, Mary Pickford

hadn't cut off her long curls until 1928. Had Irene and Vernon Castle done a silent film in, say, 1921?

Management was still calling on waving hands.

"I think we should have an espresso cart in the building," Dr. Applegate said.

"I think we should have a workout room," Elaine said.

"And some more stairs."

This could go on all day, and I wanted to check and see what movies had come out in 1922. I stood up, as unobtrusively as possible, snatched a form from Flip, who had skipped our table, and ducked out the back, leafing through the form to see how long it was.

Wonder of wonders, it was actually shorter than the original. Only twenty-two pages. And the type was only slightly smaller than— I crashed into someone and looked up.

It was Dr. O'Reilly, who must have been doing the same thing. "Sorry," he said. "I was thinking about this funding reapplication thing." He raised both hands, still holding the funding form in the right one, and faced his palms out. "Tell your partner three things you don't like about Management."

"Can it be more than three?" I said. "I suppose this means you won't get your macaques right away, Dr. O'Reilly."

"Call me Bennett," he said. "Flip's the only one with a title. I was supposed to get them this week. Now I'll have to wait till the twentieth. How about you? Does this affect your Hula Hoop project?"

"Hair-bobbing," I said. "The only effect is that I won't have any time to work on it because I'll be filling out this stupid form. I *wish* Management would find something to think about besides making up new forms."

"Shh," someone said fiercely from the door.

We moved farther down the hall, out of range.

"Paperwork is the cornerstone of Management," Bennett

whispered. "They think reducing everything to forms is the key to scientific discovery. Unfortunately science doesn't work that way. Look at Newton. Look at Archimedes."

"Management would never have approved the funding for an orchard," I agreed, "or a bathtub."

"Or a river," Bennett said. "Which is why we lost our chaos theory funding and I had to come to work for GRIM."

"What were you working on?" I asked.

"The Loue. It's a river in France. It has its source in a grotto, which means it's a small, contained system with a comparatively limited number of variables. The systems scientists have tried to study before were huge—weather, the human body, rivers. They had thousands, even millions of variables, which made them impossible to predict, so we found . . ."

Up close his tie was even more nondescript than from a distance. It appeared to have some sort of pattern, though what exactly I couldn't make out. Not paisley (which had been popular in 1988), or polka dots (1970). It wasn't a nonpattern either.

". . . and measured the air temperature, water temperature, dimensions of the grotto, makeup of the water, plant life along the banks—" he said and stopped. "You're probably busy and don't have time to listen to all this."

"That's okay," I said. "I've got to go back to my office, but I'll walk you as far as the stairs."

"Okay, well, so my idea was that by precisely measuring every factor in a chaotic system, I could isolate the causes of chaos."

"Flip," I said. "The cause of chaos."

He laughed. "The *other* causes of chaos. I know talking about the causes of chaos sounds like a contradiction in terms, since chaotic systems are supposed to be systems where ordinary cause and effect break down. They're nonlinear, which means there are so many factors, operating in such an inter-connected way, that they're impossible to predict."

Like fads, I thought.

"But there are laws governing them. We've mathemati-cally defined some of them: entropy, interior instabilities, and iteration, which is—"

"The butterfly effect," I said.

"Right. A tiny variable feeds back into the system and then the feedback feeds back, until it influences the system all out of proportion to its size."

I nodded. "A butterfly flapping its wings in L.A. can cause a typhoon in Hong Kong. Or an all-staff meeting at HiTek."

He looked delighted. "You know something about chaos?"

"Only from personal experience," I said.

"Yeah," he said, "it does seem to be the order of the day around here. Well, so, anyway, my project was to calculate the effects of iteration and entropy and see if they accounted for chaos or if there was another factor involved."

"Was there?"

He looked thoughtful. "Chaos theorists think the Heisen-berg uncertainty principle means that chaotic systems are in-herently unpredictable. Verhoest believes that prediction is possible, but he's proposed there's another force driving chaos, an X factor that's influencing its behavior."

"Moths," I said.

"What?"

"Or locusts. Something other than butterflies."

"Oh. Right. But he's wrong. My theory is that iteration can account for everything that goes on in a chaotic system, once all the factors are known and properly measured. I never got the chance to find out. We were only able to do two runs before I got my funding cut. They didn't show an increase in predictability, which means either I was wrong or I didn't have all the variables." He stopped, his hand on a door handle, and I realized we were standing outside his door. I had apparently walked him all the way down to Bio.

"Well," I said, wishing I had more time to analyze his tie, "I guess I'd better get back to work. I've got to brace myself for Flip's new assistant. And fill out my funding allocation form." I looked at it ruefully. "At least it's short."

He peered blankly at me through his thick glasses.

"Only twenty-two pages," I said, holding it up.

"The funding forms aren't printed up yet," he said. "We're supposed to get them tomorrow." He pointed at the form I was holding. "That's the new simplified supply procurement form. For ordering paper clips."

2. bubblings

Mankind, of course, always has been and always will be, under the yoke of the butterflies in the matter of social rites, dress, entertainment, and the expenditure which these things involve.

hugh shetfield, the sovereignty of society, 1909

miniature golf (1927—31)

Recreation fad of small golf courses with eighteen very short holes complicated by windmills, waterfalls, and tiny sand traps. Its popularity was easily explainable. It was a cheap place to take a Depression date, had a low skill threshold with multiple achievement levels, and let you pretend for a couple of hours that you were part of the refined country-club set. Over forty thousand courses sprang up across the country, and at its height it was so popular it was even a threat to the movies, and the studios forbade their actors to be seen playing miniature golf. Died from overexposure.

The source of the Colorado River doesn't look like one either. It's in a glacier field up in the Green River Mountains, and what it looks like is tundra and snow and rock.

But even in deepest winter there's some melting, a drop here, a trickle there, a little film of water forming at the grubby edges of the glacier and spilling over onto the frozen ground. Falling and freezing, collecting, converging, so slowly you can't see it.

Scientific research is like that, too. "Eureka!"'s like the one Archimedes had when he stepped in a bathtub and suddenly realized the answer to the problem of testing metals' density are few and far between, and mostly it's just trying and failing and trying something else, feeding in data and eliminating variables and staring at the results, trying to figure out where you went wrong.

Take Arno Penzias and Robert Wilson. Their goal was to measure the absolute intensity of radio signals from space, but first they had to get rid of the background noise in their detector.

They moved their detector to the country to get rid of city noise, radar stations, and atmospheric noise, which helped, but there was still background noise.

They tried to think what might be causing it. Birds? They went up on the roof and looked at the horn-shaped antenna. Sure enough, pigeons were nesting inside it, leaving droppings that might be causing the problem.

They evicted the pigeons, cleaned the antenna, and sealed every possible joint and crack (probably with duct tape). There was still background noise.

All right. So what else could it be? Streams of electrons from nuclear testing? If it was, the noise should be diminishing, since atomic tests had been banned in 1963. They ran dozens of tests on the intensity to see if it was. It wasn't.

And it seemed to be the same no matter which part of the heavens were overhead, which made no sense at all.

They tested and retested, taped and retaped, scraped off pigeon droppings, and despaired of ever getting to the point where they could perform their experiment on radio signal intensity for nearly five years before they realized what they had wasn't background noise at all. It was microwaves, the resounding echo of the Big Bang.

Friday Flip brought the new funding application. It was sixty-eight pages long and poorly stapled. Three pages fell out of it as Flip slouched in the door and two more as she handed it to me. "Thank you, Flip," I said, and smiled at her.

The night before I had read the last two thirds of *Pippa Passes*, during which Pippa had talked two murderously adulterous lovers into killing themselves, convinced a deceived young student to choose love over revenge, and reformed assorted ne'er-do-wells. And all just by chirping, "The year's at the spring,/And day's at the morn." Think what she could have accomplished if she'd had a library card.

"You can change the world," Browning was clearly saying. "By being perky and signaling before turning left, one person can have a positive effect on society," and it was obvious from "The Pied Piper" that he understood how trends worked.

I hadn't noticed any of these effects, but then neither had Pippa, who had presumably gone back to work at the silk factory the next day without any notion of all the good she'd done. I could see her at the staff meeting Management had called to introduce their new management system, PESTO. Right after the sensitivity exercise her coworker would lean over and whisper, "So, Pippa, what did you do on your day off?" and Pippa would shrug and say, "Nothing much. You know, hung out."

So I might be having more of an effect on literacy and left-turn signaling than I'd realized, and, by being pleasant and polite, could stop the downward trend to rudeness.

Of course, Browning had never met Flip. But it was worth a try, and I had the comfort of knowing I couldn't possibly make things worse.

So, even though Flip had made no effort to pick up the spilled pages and was, in fact, standing on one of them, I smiled at her and said, "How are you this morning?"

"Oh, just *great*," she said sarcastically. "Perfectly *fine*." She flopped down onto the hair-bobbing clippings on my lab table. "You will not *believe* what they expect me to do now!"

A little work? I thought uncharitably, and then remembered I was supposed to be following in Pippa's footsteps. "Who's they?" I said, bending to pick up the spilled pages.

"*Man*agement," she said, rolling her eyes. She was wearing a pair of neon-yellow tights, a tie-dyed T-shirt, and a very peculiar down vest. It was short and bunched oddly around the neck and armpits. "You know how I'm supposed to get a new job title and an assistant?"

"Yes," I said, continuing to smile. "Did you? Get a new job title?"

"*Ye-es*," she said. "I'm the interdepartmental communications liaison. But for my assistant, they expect me to be on a *search* committee. *After* work."

Along the bottom of the vest there was a row of snaps, a style I had never seen before. She's wearing it upside down, I thought.

"The whole *point* was I was overworked. That's why I have to have an assistant, isn't it? Hel*lo*?"

Wearing clothing some other way than was intended is an ever-popular variety of fad—untied shoelaces, backward baseball caps, ties for belts, slips for dresses—and one that can't be put down to merchandising because it doesn't cost anything. It's not new, either. High school girls in 1955 took to wearing their cardigan sweaters backward, and their mothers had worn unbuckled galoshes with short skirts and raccoon coats in the 1920s. The metal buckles had jangled and flapped, which is how the name *flapper* came about. Or, since there doesn't seem to be agreement on the source of anything where fads are concerned, they were named for the chickenlike flapping of their arms when they did the Charleston. But the Charleston didn't hit till 1923, and the word *flapper* had been used as early as 1920.

"*Well*," Flip said. "Do you want to hear this or not?"

It was no wonder Pippa had just gone singing past her clients' windows. If she'd had to put up with them, she wouldn't have been half as cheerful. I forced an interested expression. "Who else is on the committee?"

"*I* don't know. I told you, I don't have time to go to these things."

"But don't you want to make sure you get a good assistant?"

"Not if I have to stay after work," she said, irritably pulling clippings out from under her. "Your office is a mess. Don't you ever clean it?"

" 'The lark's on the wing;/The snail's on the thorn,' " I said.

"*What?*"

So Browning was wrong. "I'd love to talk," I said, "but I'd better get started on this funding form."

She didn't show any signs of moving. She was looking aimlessly through the clippings.

"I need you to make a copy of each of those. Now. Before you go to your search committee meeting."

Still nothing. I got a pencil, stuck the extra pages into the application, and tried to focus on the simplified funding form.

I never worry much about getting funding. It's true there are fads in both science and industry, but greed is always in style. HiTek would like nothing more than to know what causes fads so they could invent the next one. And stats projects are cheap. The only funding I was requesting was for a computer with more memory capacity. Which didn't mean I could forget about the funding form. It wouldn't matter if your project was a sure-fire method for turning lead into gold, if you don't have the forms filled out *and* turned in on time, Management will cancel you like a shot.

Project goals, experimental method, projected results, matrix analysis ranking. Matrix analysis ranking?

I flipped the page over to see if there were instructions, and the page came out altogether. There weren't any instructions, there or at the end of the application. "Were there instructions included with the form?" I asked Flip.

"How would I know?" she said, getting up. "What's this?" She stuck one of the clippings under my nose, an ad of a bobbed blonde standing next to a Hupmobile.

"The car?"

"No-o-o," she said, letting her breath out in a big sigh. "Her *hair*."

"A bob," I said, and leaned closer to see if the hair was cut in an Eton bob or a shingle. It was crimped in even rows down the sides of her head. "A marcel wave," I said. "It was a permanent wave done with a special electrical metal-and-wires apparatus that was about as much fun as going to the dentist," but Flip had already lost interest.

"I think if they're going to make you stay after work or make you do extra jobs they should pay you overtime. Like stapling all these funding forms and delivering them to everybody. Some of them were supposed to go all the way down to Bio."

"Did you deliver one to Dr. O'Reilly?" I said, remembering her habit of dumping packages on closer offices.

"Of *course*. He didn't even thank me. What a swarb!"

"Swarb?" I said. Fads in language are impossible to keep up with, and I don't even try from a research standpoint, but I know most of the slang because that's how fads are described. But I'd never heard this one.

"You don't know what *swarb* means?" she said, in a tone that made me wish Pippa had gone around Italy slapping people. "No hots. No cutes. Cyber-ugg. Swarb." She flailed her duct-taped arms, trying to think of the word. "*Completely* fashion-impaired," she said, and flounced out in her duct tape and upside-down down. Without the clippings.

coffeehouse (1450—1554) Middle Eastern fad that originated in Aden, then spread to Mecca and throughout Persia and Turkey. Men sat cross-legged on rugs and sipped thick, black, bitter coffee from tiny cups while listening to poets. The coffeehouses eventually became more popular than mosques and were banned by the religious authorities, who claimed they were frequented by people "of low costume and very little industry." Spread to London (1652), Paris (1669), Boston (1675), Seattle (1985).

Saturday morning the library called and told me my name had come up on the reserve list for *Led On by Fate*, so I went to Boulder to pick it up and buy a birthday present for Brittany.

"You can have *Angels, Angels Everywhere*, too, if you want," Lorraine told me at the library. She was wearing a sweatshirt with a dalmatian on it and red fireplug earrings. "We *finally* got two more copies now that nobody wants them."

I leafed through it while she swiped *Led On by Fate* with the light pen.

"Your guardian angel goes with you everywhere," it said. "It's always there, right beside you, wherever you go." There was a line drawing of an angel with large wings looming over a woman in a grocery checkout line. "You can ignore them, you can even pretend they don't exist, but that won't make them go away."

Until the fad's over, I thought.

I checked out *Led On by Fate* and a book on chaos theory and Mandelbrot diagrams so I'd have a pretext for going down to Bio to see what Dr. O'Reilly was wearing, and went over to the Pearl Street Mall.

Lorraine was right. The bookstore had *Angel in My Condo* and *The Cherubim Cookbook* on a sale rack, and *The Angel Calendar* was marked fifty percent off. There was a big display up front for *Faerie Encounters of the Fourth Kind.*

I went upstairs to the kids' section and more fairies: *The Flower Fairies* (which had been a fad once before, back in the 1910s); *Fairies, Fairies Everywhere; More Fairies, Fairies Everywhere;* and *The Land of Faerie Fun.* Also Batman books, *Lion King* books, Power Rangers books, and Barbie books.

I finally managed to find a hardback copy of *Toads and Diamonds,* which I'd loved as a kid. It had a fairy in it, but not like those in *Fairies, Fairies, Etc.*, with lavender wings and bluebells for hats. It was about a girl who helps an ugly old woman who turns out to be a good fairy in disguise. Inner values versus shallow appearances. My kind of moral.

I bought it and went out into the mall. It was a beautiful Indian summer day, balmy and blue-skied. The Pearl Street Mall on a Saturday's a great place to analyze trends, since, one, there are hordes of people, and two, Boulder's almost terminally hip. The rest of the state calls it the People's Republic of Boulder, and it's got every possible kind of New Ager and falafel stand and street musician.

There are even fads in street music. Guitars were out and bongos were in again. (The first time was in 1958, at the height of the Beat movement. Very low ability threshold.) Flip's buzzcut-and-swag was very in, and so was the buzzcut-

and-message. And duct tape. I saw two people with strips around their sleeves and one with dreadlocks and a bowler had a wide band of duct tape wrapped around his neck like the ones the French had worn during the *à la victime* fad after the Revolution.

Which was incidentally the last time women had cut their hair short until the 1920s, and it was a snap to trace that fad to its source. Aristocrats had had their hair chopped off to make it easier on the guillotine, and after the Empire was reinstated, relatives and friends had worn their hair short in sympathetic tribute. They'd also tied narrow red ribbons around their necks, but I doubted if that was what the dreadlocks person had had in mind. Or maybe it was.

Backpacks were out, and tiny, dangling wallets-on-a-string were in. Also Ugg boots, and kneeless jeans, and plaid flannel shirts. There wasn't an inch of corduroy anywhere. In-line skating with no regard for human life was very much in, as was walking slowly and obliviously four abreast. Sunflowers were out and violets were in. Ditto the Sinéad O'Connor look, and hair wraps. The long, thin strands of hair wrapped in brightly colored thread were everywhere.

Crystals and aromatherapy were out, replaced apparently by recreational ethnicity. The New Age shops were advertising Iroquois sweat lodges, Russian banya therapy, and Peruvian vision quests, $249 double occupancy, meals included. There were two Ethiopian restaurants, a Filipino deli, and a cart selling Navajo fry bread.

And half a dozen coffeehouses, which had apparently sprung up like mushrooms overnight: the Jumpstart, the Espresso Espress, the Caffe Lottie, the Cup o' Joe, and the Caffe Java.

After a while I got tired of dodging mimes and in-line skaters and went into the Mother Earth, which was now calling itself the Caffe Krakatoa (east of Java). It was as crowded inside as it had been out on the mall. A waitress with a swag haircut was taking names. "Do you want to sit at the communal table?" she was asking the guy in front of me, pointing to a long table with two people at it, one at each end.

That's a trend that's moved over here from England, where strangers have to share tables in order to keep up with the gossip on Prince Charles and Camilla. It hasn't caught on particularly over here, where strangers are more apt to want to talk about Rush Limbaugh or their hair implants.

I had sat at communal tables a few times when they were first introduced, thinking it was a good way to get exposure to trends in language and thought, but a taste was more than enough. Just because people are experiencing things doesn't mean they have any insight into them, a fact the talk shows (a trend that has reached the cancerous uncontrolled growth stage and should shortly exhaust its food supply) should have figured out by now.

The guy was asking, "If I don't sit at the communal table, how long a wait?"

The waitress sighed. "*I* don't know. Forty minutes?" and I certainly hoped that wasn't going to be a trend.

"How *many*?" she said to me.

"Two," I said, so I wouldn't have to sit at the communal table. "Foster."

"It has to be your first name."

"Why?" I said.

She rolled her eyes. "So I can *call* you."

"Sandra," I said.

"How do you spell that?"

No, I thought, please tell me Flip isn't becoming a trend. Please.

I spelled *Sandra* for her, grabbed up the alternative newspapers, and settled into a corner for the duration. There was no point in trying to do the personals till I was at a table, but the articles were almost as good. There was a new laser technology for removing tattoos, Berkeley had outlawed smoking outdoors, the must-have color for spring was postmodern pink, and marriage was coming back in style. "Living together is passé," assorted Hollywood actresses were quoted as saying. "The cool thing now is diamond rings, weddings, commitment, the whole bit."

"Susie," the waitress called.

No one answered.

"Susie, party of two," she said, flipping her rattail. "*Susie.*"

I decided it was either me or somebody who'd given up and left. "Here," I said, and let a waiter with a Three Stooges haircut lead me to a knee-mashing table by the window. "I'm ready to order," I said before he could leave.

"I thought there were two in your party," he said.

"The other person will be here soon. I'll have a double tall caffè latte with skim milk and semisweet chocolate on top," I said brightly.

The waiter sighed and looked expectant.

"With brown sugar on the side," I said.

He rolled his eyes. "Sumatra, Yergacheffe, or Sulawesi?" he said.

I looked to the menu for help, but there was nothing there but a quote from Kahlil Gibran. "Sumatra," I said, since I knew where it was.

He sighed. "Seattle- or California-style?"

"Seattle," I said.

"With?"

"A spoon?" I said hopefully.

He rolled his eyes.

"What flavor *syrup*?"

Maple? I thought, even though that seemed unlikely. "Raspberry?" I said.

That was apparently one of the choices. He slouched off,

and I attacked the personals. There was no point in circling the NSs. They were in virtually every ad. Two had it in their headline, and one, placed by a very intelligent, strikingly handsome athlete, had it listed twice.

Friends was out, and soul work was in. There were two references to fairies, and yet another abbreviation: GC. "JSDM seeks WSNSF. Must be GC. South of Baseline. West of Twenty-eighth." I circled it and turned back to the code book. Geographically compatible.

There weren't any other GCs, but there was a "Boulder mall area preferred," and one that specified, "Valmont or Pearl, 2500 block only."

Yes, in an eight-and-a-half narrow, and I'd like that delivered Federal Express to my door. It made me think fondly of Billy Ray, who was willing to drive all the way down from Laramie to take me out.

"This place is so *ridiculous*," Flip said, sitting down across from me. She was wearing a babydoll dress, thigh-high pink stockings, and a pair of clunky Mary Janes, all of which she had on more or less right side up. "There's a forty-minute line."

Yes, I thought, and you should be in it. "There's a communal table," I said.

"*No*body sits together except swarbs and boofs," she said. "Brine made us sit at the communal table once." She bent over to pull up her thigh-highs.

There was no duct tape in evidence. Flip motioned the waiter over and ordered. "LattemarchianoskimtallJazula and not too much foam." She turned to look at me. "Brine ordered a latte with Su*ma*tra." She picked up my sack from the bookstore. "What's this?"

"A birthday present for Dr. Damati's little girl."

She had already pulled it out and was examining it curiously.

"It's a book," I said.

"Didn't they have the video?" She stuck it back in the sack. "*I* would've bought her a Barbie." She tossed her swath of hair, and I could see that she had a strip of duct tape across her forehead. There was a cut-out circle in the middle with what looked like a lowercase *i* tattooed right between her eyes.

"What's your tattoo?"

"It's not a tattoo," she said, brushing her hair back so I could see it better. It *was* a lowercase *i*. "*No*body wears tattoos anymore."

I started to draw her attention to her snowy owl and noticed that she was wearing duct tape there, too, a small circular patch right where the snowy owl had been.

"Tattoos are arti*ficial*. Sticking all those chemicals and cancerinogens under your skin," she said. "It's a brand."

"A brand," I said, wishing, as usual, that I hadn't started this.

"Brands are organic. You're not injecting something *into* your body. You're bringing out something that's already there in your natural body. Fire's one of the four elements, you know."

Sarah, over in Chem, would love to hear that.

"I've never seen one before," I said. "What does the *i* stand for?"

She looked confused. "Stand for? It doesn't stand for anything. It's *I*. You know, me. Who I am. It's a personal statement."

I decided not to ask her why her brand was lowercase, or if it had occurred to her that anyone seeing her with it would immediately assume it stood for *incompetent*.

"It's 'I,'" she said. "A person who doesn't need anybody else, especially not a *swarb* who would sit at the communal table and order Sumatra." She sighed deeply.

The waiter brought our lattes in Alice-in-Wonderland–

sized cups, which might be a trend but was probably just a practical adjustment. Pouring steaming liquids into clear glass can have disastrous results.

Flip sighed again, a huge sigh, and licked the foam despondently off the back of her long-handled spoon.

"Do you ever feel com*plete*ly itch?"

Since I had no idea what *itch* was, I licked the back of my own spoon and hoped the question was rhetorical.

It was. "I mean, like take today. Here it is, the weekend, and I'm stuck sitting here with you." Here she rolled her eyes and sighed again. "Guys suck, you know."

By which I took it she meant Brine, of the bovver boots and assorted studs.

"*Life* sucks. You say to yourself, What am I doing in my job?"

Not much, I thought.

"So, everything sucks. You're not going anywhere, you're not accomplishing anything. I'm *twenty-two*!" She ate a spoonful of foam. "Like, why can't I ever meet a guy who isn't a swarb?"

It might be the forehead tattoo, I thought, and then remembered I wasn't any better off than Flip.

"It's just like Groupthink says." She looked at me expectantly, and then expelled so much air I thought she was going to deflate. "How can you not know about Groupthink? They're the most in band in Seattle. It's like their song says, 'Spinning my wheels on the launchpad, spitting I dunno and itch.' This is too bumming," she said, glaring at me like it was my fault. "I gotta get out of here."

She snatched up her check and slouched off through the crowd toward our waiter.

After a minute he came over and handed the check to me. "Your friend said you'd pay this," he said. "She said to tip me twenty percent."

alice blue———(1902—4)——— Color fad inspired by President Teddy Roosevelt's pretty and vivacious teenage daughter, of whom her father once said, "I can be President of the United States, or I can control Alice. I cannot possibly do both." Alice Roosevelt was one of the first "media stars"; her every move, comment, and outfit was copied by an eager public. When a dress was designed for her to match her gray-blue eyes, reporters dubbed it Alice blue, and the color became instantly popular. The musical comedy *Irene* featured a song called "Alice Blue Gown," shops marketed gray-blue fabric, hats, and hair ribbons, and hundreds of babies were named Alice and dressed not in the traditional pink but in Alice blue.

· After Flip left I went back to the personals, but they seemed sad and a little desperate: "Lonely SWF seeks someone who really understands."

I wandered down the mall, looking at fairy T-shirts, fairy pillows, fairy soaps, and a cologne in a flower-shaped bottle called Elfmaiden. The Paper Doll had fairy greeting cards, fairy calendars, and fairy wrapping paper. The Peppercorn had a fairy teapot. The Quilted Unicorn, combining several trends, featured a caffè latte cup painted with a fairy dressed as a violet.

The sun had disappeared, and the day had turned gray and chilly. It looked as if it might even start to snow. I walked down past the Latte Lenya to the Fashion Front and went in to get warm and to see what color postmodern pink was.

Color fads are usually the result of a technological break-through. Mauve and turquoise, *the* colors of the 1870s, were brought about by a scientific breakthrough in the manufacture of dyes. So were the Day-Glo colors of the 1960s. And the new jewel-tone maroon and emerald car colors.

The fact that new colors are few and far between has never stopped fashion designers, though. They just give a new name to an old color. Like Schiaparelli's "shocking" pink in the 1920s, and Chanel's "beige" for what had previously been a nondescript tan. Or name a color after somebody, whether they wore it or not, like Victoria blue, Victoria green, Victoria red, and the ever-popular, and a lot more logical, Victoria black.

The clerk in the Fashion Front was talking on the phone to her boyfriend and examining her split ends. "Do you have postmodern pink?" I said.

"*Yeah,*" she said belligerently, and turned back to the phone. "I have to go wait on this *woman,*" she said, slammed the phone down, and slouched over to the racks.

It is a fad, I thought, following her. Flip is a fad.

She shoved past a counter full of angel sweatshirts marked seventy-five percent off, and gestured at the rack. "And it's po-mo pink," she said, rolling her eyes. "Not postmodern."

"It's supposed to be the hot color for fall," I said.

"Whatever," she said, and slouched back to the phone while I examined "the hottest new color to hit since the six-ties."

It wasn't new. It had been called ashes-of-roses the first time around in 1928 and dove pink the second in 1954.

Both times it had been a grim, grayish pink that washed

out skin and hair, which hadn't stopped it from being hugely popular. It no doubt would be again in its present incarnation as po-mo pink.

It wasn't as good a name as ashes-of-roses, but names don't have to be enticing to be faddish. Witness flea, the winning color of 1776. And the hit of Louis XVI's court had been, I'm not kidding, puce. And not just plain puce. It had been so popular it'd come in a whole variety of appetizing shades: young puce, old puce, puce-belly, puce-thigh, and puce-with-milk-fever.

I bought a three-foot-long piece of po-mo pink ribbon to take back to the lab, which meant the clerk had to get off the phone *again*. "This is for hair wraps," she said, looking disapprovingly at my short hair, and gave me the wrong change.

"Do you like po-mo pink?" I asked her.

She sighed. "It's *the* boss color for fall."

Of course. And therein lay the secret to all fads: the herd instinct. People wanted to look like everybody else. That was why they bought white bucks and pedal pushers and bikinis. But someone had to be the first one to wear platform shoes, to bob their hair, and that took the opposite of herd instinct.

I put my incorrect change and my ribbon in my shoulder bag (very passé) and went back out onto the mall. It had started to spit snow and the street musicians were shivering in their Birkenstocks and Ecuador shirts. I put on my mittens (com*plete*ly swarb) and walked back down toward the library, looking at yuppie shops and bagel stands and getting more and more depressed. I had no idea where any of these fads came from, even po-mo pink, which some fashion designer had come up with. But the fashion designer couldn't make people buy po-mo pink, couldn't make them wear it and make jokes about it and write editorials on the subject of "What is fashion coming to?"

The fashion designers could make it popular this season,

especially since nobody would be able to find anything else in the stores, but they couldn't make it a fad. In 1971, they'd tried to introduce the long midiskirt and failed utterly, and they'd been predicting the "comeback of the hat" for years to no avail. It took more than merchandising to make a fad, and I didn't have any idea what that something more was.

And the more I fed in my data, the more convinced I was the answer wasn't in it, that increased independence and lice and bicycling were nothing more than excuses, reasons thought up afterward to explain what no one understood. Especially me.

I wondered if I was even in the right field. I was feeling so dissatisfied, as if everything I was doing was pointless, so . . . itch.

Flip, I thought. She did this to me with her talk about Brine and Groupthink. She's some kind of anti–guardian angel, following me everywhere, hindering rather than helping and putting me in a bad mood. And I'm not going to let her ruin my weekend. It's bad enough she ruins the rest of the week.

I bought a piece of chocolate cheesecake and went back to the library and checked out *The Red Badge of Courage*, *How Green Was My Valley*, and *The Color Purple*, but the mood persisted throughout the steely afternoon, and all the icy way home, making it impossible for me to work.

I tried reading the chaos theory book I'd checked out, but it just made me more depressed. Chaotic systems had so many variables it would have been nearly impossible to predict the systems' behavior if they acted in logical, straightforward ways. But they didn't.

Every variable interacted with every other, colliding and connecting in unexpected ways, setting up iteration loops that fed into the system again and again, crisscrossing and connecting the variables so many ways it wasn't surprising a butterfly could have a devastating effect. Or none at all.

I could see why Dr. O'Reilly had wanted to study a system with limited variables, but what was limited? According to the book, anything and everything was a variable: entropy, gravity, the quantum effects of an electron, or a star on the other side of the universe.

So even if Dr. O'Reilly was right and there weren't any outside X factors operating on the system, there was no way to compute all the variables or even decide what they were.

It all bore an uncomfortable resemblance to fads and made me wonder which variables I wasn't taking into account, so that when Billy Ray called, I clutched at him like a drowning man. "I'm so glad you called," I said. "My research went faster than I thought it would, so I'm free after all. Where are you?"

"On my way to Bozeman," he said. "When you said you were busy, I decided to skip the seminar and go pick up those Targhees I was looking at." He paused, and I could hear the warning hum of his cell phone. "I'll be back on Monday. How about dinner sometime next week?"

I wanted dinner tonight, I thought crabbily. "Great," I said. "Call me when you get back."

The hum crescendoed. "Sorry we missed each oth—" he said and went out of range.

I went and looked out the window at the sleet and then got into bed and read *Led On by Fate* cover to cover, which wasn't much of a feat. It was only ninety-four pages long, and so obviously wretchedly written it was destined to become a huge fad.

Its premise was that everything was ordained and organized by guardian angels, and the heroine was given to saying things like "Everything happens for a *reason*, Derek! You broke off our engagement and slept with Edwina and were implicated in her death, and I turned to Paolo for comfort and went to Nepal with him so that we'd learn the meaning of suffering and despair, without which true love is meaningless. All of it—the train wreck, Lilith's suicide, Halvard's drug addiction, the stock market crash—it was all so we could be together. Oh, Derek, there's a reason behind everything!"

Except, apparently, hair-bobbing. I woke up at three with Irene Castle and golf clubs dancing in my head. That happened to Henri Poincaré. He'd been working on mathematical functions for days and days, and one night he drank too much coffee (which probably had had the same effect as bad literature) and couldn't sleep, and mathematical ideas "rose in crowds."

And Friedrich Kekulé. He'd fallen into a reverie on top of a bus and seen chains of carbon atoms dancing wildly around. One of the chains had suddenly taken its tail in its mouth and formed a ring, and Kekulé had ended up discovering the benzene ring and revolutionizing organic chemistry.

All Irene Castle did with the golf clubs was the hesitation waltz, and after a while I turned on the light and opened Browning.

It turned out he had known Flip after all. He'd written a poem, "Soliloquy of the Spanish Cloister," about her. "G-r-r, you swine," he'd written, obviously after she crumpled up all his poems, and "There go, my heart's abhorrence." I decided to say it to Flip the next time she stuck me with the check.

hot pants (1971)——Fashion fad worn by everyone that only looked good on the very young and shapely. A successor to the miniskirt of the sixties, hot pants were a reaction to fashion designers' attempts to introduce the midcalf-length midiskirt. Hot pants were made out of satin or velvet, often with suspenders, and were worn with patent leather boots. Women wore them to the office, and they were even allowed in the Miss America pageant.

I spent the rest of the weekend ironing clippings and trying to decipher the simplified funding allocation form. What were Thrust Overlay Parameters? And my Efficiency Prioritization Ranking? And what did they mean by "List proprietary site bracket restrictions"? It made looking for the cause of hair-bobbing (or the source of the Nile) seem like a breeze in comparison.

Nobody else knew what EDI endorsements were either. When I went to work Monday, everybody I knew came up to the stats lab to ask about it.

"Do you have any idea how to fill this stupid funding form out?" Sarah asked, sticking her head in the door at midmorning.

"Nope," I said.

"What do you suppose an expense gradation index is?" She leaned against the door. "Do you ever feel like you should just give up and start over?"

Yes, I thought, looking at my computer screen. I had spent most of the morning reading clippings, extracting what I hoped was the relevant information from them, typing it onto a disk, and designing statistical programs to interpret it. Or what Billy Ray had referred to as "sticking it on the computer and pushing a button."

I'd pushed the button, and surprise, surprise, there were no surprises. There was a correlation between the number of women in the workforce and the number of outraged references to hair-bobbing in the newspapers, an even stronger one between bobs and cigarette sales, and no correlation between the length of hair and the length of skirts, which I could have predicted. Skirts had dipped back to midcalf in 1926, while hair had gone steadily shorter all the way to the crash of '29, with the boyish shingle in 1925 and the even shorter Eton crop in 1926.

The strongest correlation of all was to the cloche hat, thus giving support to the cart-before-the-horse theory and proving beyond a shadow of a doubt that statistics isn't all that it's cracked up to be.

"Lately I've been feeling depressed about the whole thing," Sarah was saying. "I've always believed it was just a question of his having a higher relationship threshold than I do, but I've been thinking maybe this is just part of the denial structure that goes with codependent relationships."

Ted, I thought. We're talking about Ted, who doesn't want to get married.

"And this weekend, I got to thinking, What's the point? I'm following an intimacy path and he's into off-road detachment."

"Itch," I said.

"What?"

"What you're feeling," I said. "Like you're spinning your wheels on the launchpad. You didn't run into Flip this weekend, did you?"

"I saw her this morning," she said. "She brought me Dr. Applegate's mail."

An antiangel, wandering through the world spreading gloom and destruction.

"Well, anyway," Sarah said, "I'd better go see if I can find somebody in Management who can tell me what an expense gradation index is," and left.

I went back to my hair-bobbing data. I ran a geographical distribution for 1923 and then for 1922. They showed clusters in New York City and Hollywood, which were no surprise, and St. Paul, Minnesota, and Marydale, Ohio, which were. On a hunch, I asked for a breakdown of Montgomery, Alabama. It showed a cluster too small to be statistically significant but enough to explain the St. Paul one. Montgomery was where F. Scott Fitzgerald had met Zelda, and St. Paul was his hometown. The locals obviously were trying to live up to "Bernice Bobs Her Hair." It didn't explain Marydale, Ohio. I ran a geographical distribution for 1921. It was still there.

"*Here,*" Flip said, sticking my mail under my nose. Apparently nobody had told her po-mo pink was the in color for fall. She was wearing a brilliant bilious blue tunic and leggings and an assortment of duct tape.

"I'm glad you're here," I said, grabbing a stack of clippings. "You owe me two-fifty for your caffè latte and I need you to copy these for me. Oh, and wait." I went and got the personals I'd gone through Saturday, and two articles about angels. I handed them to Flip. "One copy of each."

"I don't believe in angels," she said.

Right on the cutting edge, as usual.

"I used to believe in them," she said, "but I don't anymore, not since Brine. I mean, if you really had a guardian angel, she'd cheer you up when you were bummed and get you out of committee meetings and stuff."

"What about fairies?" I asked.

"You mean like fairy godmothers?" she said. "Of course. Duh."

Of course.

I went back to my hair-bobbing. Marydale, Ohio. What could it have had to make it a hot spot of hair-bobbing? Hot, I thought. How about unusually hot weather in Ohio during the summer of 1921? So hot long hair would have clung sweatily to the back of the neck, and women would have said, "I can't take this anymore"?

I called up weather data for the state of Ohio for June through September and began looking for Marydale.

"Do you have a minute?" said a voice from the door. It was Elaine from Personnel. She was wearing a sweatband and a sour expression. "Do you have any idea what hiral implementation format rations are?" she asked.

"Not a clue. Did you try Management?"

"I've been up there twice and couldn't get in. There's a huge crowd." She took a deep breath. "I'm getting totally stressed. Do you want to go work out?"

"Stair-climbing?" I said dubiously.

She shook her head firmly. "Stair-climbing doesn't give a large-muscle workout. Wall-walking. Gym over on Twenty-eighth. They've got pitons and everything."

"No, thanks," I said. "I've got walls here."

She looked disapprovingly at them and went out, and I went back to my hair-bobbing. 1921 temps for Marydale had been slightly lower than normal, and it wasn't the hometown of either Irene Castle or Isadora Duncan.

I abandoned it for the moment and did a Pareto chart and

then ran some more regressions. There was a weak correlation between church attendance and bobs, a strong correlation between bobs and Hupmobile sales, but not Packards or Model T Fords, and a very strong correlation between bobs and women in nursing careers. I called up a list of American hospitals in 1921. There wasn't one within a hundred miles of Marydale.

Gina came in, looking harassed.

"No, I don't know how to fill out the funding form," I said before she could ask, "and neither does anybody else."

"Really?" she said vaguely. "I haven't even looked at it yet. I've been spending all my time on the stupid search committee for Flip's assistant. What do *you* consider the most important quality in an assistant?"

"Being the opposite of Flip," I said, and then, when she didn't laugh, "Competence, cheerfulness, willingness to work?"

"Exactly," she said. "And if a person had those qualities, you'd hire them immediately, wouldn't you? And if they were as overqualified for the job as she is, you'd snap them right up. You wouldn't turn her down because of one little drawback and expect them to interview dozens of other people, especially when you've got other things to do. Fill out this ridiculous funding form, for one, *and* plan a birthday party. Do you know what Brittany picked, when I said she couldn't have the Power Rangers? *Barney.* And it isn't as if she isn't competent *and* cheerful *and* willing to work. Right?"

I was unclear as to whether she was talking about Brittany or the assistant applicant. "Barney is pretty awful," I said.

"Exactly," Gina said, as if I'd proved her point, whatever it was. "I'm hiring her," and she flounced out.

I went back and sat down in front of the computer. Cloche hats, Hupmobiles, and Marydale, Ohio. None of them seemed likely to be the trigger. What was? What had suddenly set the fad in motion?

Flip came in, carrying the stack of clippings and personals I'd just given her. "What did you want me to do with these again?"

mesmerism (1778—84) Scientific fad resulting from new discoveries about magnetism, speculation about its medical possibilities, and greed. Paris society flocked to Dr. Mesmer to have "animal magnetism" treatments involving tubs of "magnetized water," iron rods, and Dr. Mesmer's lavender-robed assistants, who massaged the patients and looked deep into their eyes. The patients screamed, sobbed, sank into a deep trance, and paid Dr. Mesmer on leaving. Actually hypnotism, animal magnetism claimed to cure everything from tumors to consumption. Died out when a scientific investigation headed by Ben Franklin proved it did no such thing.

Tuesday Management called another meeting. "To explain the simplified funding forms," I said to Gina, walking down to the cafeteria.

"I hope so," she said, looking even more harassed than she had yesterday. "It would be nice to see somebody else on the defensive for a change."

I was going to ask her what she meant by that, but just then I spotted Dr. O'Reilly on the far side of the room talking to Dr. Turnbull. She was wearing a po-mo pink suit (sans shoulder pads), and he had on one of those print polyester shirts from the seventies. By the time I'd taken all that in, Gina was at our table with Sarah, Elaine, and a bunch of other people.

I walked over, bracing myself for a discussion of intimacy issues and power-walking, but they were apparently discussing Flip's new assistant.

"I didn't think it was possible to hire somebody worse than Flip," Elaine was saying. "How *could* you, Gina?"

"But she's very competent," Gina said defensively. "She's had experience with Windows and SPSS, and she knows how to repair a copy machine."

"All that's entirely irrelevant," a woman from Physics said, though it didn't sound irrelevant to me.

"Well, *I'm* not working with her," a man from Product Development said. "And don't tell me you didn't know she was one. You can tell just by looking at her."

Bigotry is one of the oldest and ugliest of trends, so persistent it only counts as a fad because the target keeps changing: Huguenots, Koreans, homosexuals, Muslims, Tutsis, Jews, Quakers, wolves, Serbs, Salem housewives. Nearly every group, so long as it's small and different, has had a turn, and the pattern never changes—disapproval, isolation, demonization, persecution. Which was one of the reasons it'd be nice to find the switch that turned fads on. I'd like to turn that one off for good.

"People like that shouldn't be allowed to work in a big company like HiTek," Sarah, who was actually a nice person in spite of her psychobabble about Ted, was saying.

And Dr. Applegate, who definitely should know better, added disgustedly, "I suppose if you fired her, she'd sue for discrimination. That's what's wrong with all this affirmative action stuff."

I wondered what small and different group Flip's new assistant had the misfortune to belong to: Hispanic, lesbian, NRA member?

"She's not setting foot in my lab," a woman wearing a turban said. "I'm not exposing myself to unnecessary health risks."

"But she won't be smoking on the job," Gina said. "She can keyboard a hundred words a minute."

"I can't believe I'm hearing this," Elaine said. "Haven't you read the FDA report on the dangers of secondhand smoke?"

On the other hand, there are moments when rather than reforming the human race I'd like to abandon it altogether and go become, say, one of Dr. O'Reilly's macaques, which have to have more sense.

I was about to say as much to Elaine when Dr. O'Reilly grabbed my arm. "Come sit with me," he said, and led me away. "I need you to be my partner in case Management springs another sensitivity thing." He looked at me uncertainly. "Unless you'd rather sit with your friends."

"No," I said, watching them surround Gina. "Not at the moment."

"Oh, good," he said. "The last sensitivity exercise, I got stuck with Flip." We sat down. "So how's your fads research coming?"

"It's not," I said. "I picked hair-bobbing because I wanted a fad that didn't have an obvious cause. Most fads are caused by a breakthrough in technology—nylons, waterbeds, light-up sneakers."

"Fallout shelters."

I nodded. "Or they're a marketing phenomena, like Trivial Pursuit and teddy bears."

"And fallout shelters."

"Right. Hair-bobbing didn't cost anything except the bar-

ber's fee, and if you didn't have that, all you needed to whack
your hair off was a pair of scissors, which is a technology that's
been around forever." I started to sigh and then realized I'd
sound like Flip.

"So what's the problem?" Bennett asked.

"The problem is hair-bobbing doesn't have an obvious
cause. Irene Castle looked like a possibility for a while, but it
turned out she was following a Dutch bob fad that had been
popular in Paris the year before. And none of the other
sources has a direct correlation to the critical period. Have
you ever heard of a place called Marydale, Ohio?"

"Good *morn*ing," Management said from the podium. He
was wearing a polo shirt, Dockers, and a pleased smile. "We're
really excited to see you all here."

"What's Management up to?" I whispered to Bennett.

"My guess is a new acronym," he whispered. "Departmental Unification Management Business." He wrote down
the letters on his legal pad. "D.U.M.B."

"We have several items of business today," Management
said happily. "First, some of you have been having minor diffi-
culties filling out the simplified funding allocation forms.
You'll be receiving a memo that answers all your questions.
The interdepartmental communications liaison is in the process of making copies for each of you right now."

Bennett put his head down on the table.

"Secondly, I'd like to announce that HiTek is instituting a
'dress down' policy beginning this week. This is an innovative
idea that all the best corporations are implementing. Casual
dress induces a more relaxed workplace and stronger interem-
ployee interfaces. So starting tomorrow I'll expect to see all of
you in casual clothes."

I tuned him out and studied Bennett. He looked terrible.
His polyester print shirt had little daisies on it in an assort-

ment of browns, none of which came close to matching his brown cords. Over it he was wearing a pilled gray cardigan.

But it wasn't just the clothes. *The Brady Bunch Movie* had made seventies styles fashionable again. Flip had worn satin disco pants the other day, and platform shoes and gold chains were all over the Boulder mall. But Bennett didn't look "retro." He looked "swarb." I had the feeling that if he were wearing a bomber jacket and Nikes he'd still look that way. As if he were an antifaddist.

No, that wasn't right either. Any number of fads were started as a rejection of existing fads. The long hair of the sixties was a rejection of the crew cuts of the fifties, the short, flat, figureless flapper dresses a reaction to the exaggeratedly bustled and corseted Victorians.

Bennett wasn't rebelling. It was more like he was oblivious to the whole concept. No, that wasn't the right word either. Immune.

And if he could be immune to fads, did that mean they were caused by some kind of virus? I looked over at Gina's table, where Elaine and Dr. Applegate were earnestly whispering to her about emphysema and the surgeon general's warning. Was Bennett really immune to fads or just fashion-impaired, as Flip had said?

I opened my notebook and wrote, "They hired Flip's new assistant," and pushed it over in front of him.

He wrote back, "I know. I met her this morning. Her name's Shirl."

"Did you know she smokes?" I wrote and watched his expression when he read it. He looked neither surprised nor repelled.

"Flip told me," he wrote. "She said Shirl was going to pollute the workplace. The pot calling the kettle black."

I grinned.

"What does that *i* tattoo on Flip's forehead stand for?" he wrote.

"It's not a tattoo, it's a brand," I wrote back.

"*Incompetent* or *impossible*?"

"Initiative," Management said, and we both looked up guiltily. "Which brings me to our third item of business. How many of you know what the Niebnitz Grant is?"

I did, and even though nobody else raised their hand, I was willing to bet everybody else did, too. It's the largest research grant there is, even bigger than the MacArthur Grant, and with virtually no strings attached. The scientist gets the money and can apply it to any kind of research at all. Or retire to the Bahamas.

It's also the most mysterious research grant there is. Nobody knows who gives it, what they give it for, or even when it's given. There was one awarded last year, to Lawrence Chin, an artificial intelligence researcher, four the year before that, and none before that for over three years. The Niebnitz people (whoever they are) sweep down periodically like one of those Angels from Above on some unsuspecting scientist and make it so he never has to fill out another simplified funding allocation form.

There are no requirements, no application form, no particular field of study the grant favors. Of the four the year before last, one was a Nobel prize winner, one a graduate assistant, one a chemist at a French research institute, and one a part-time inventor. The only thing that's known for sure is the amount, which Management had just written on his flipchart: $1,000,000.

"The winner of the Niebnitz Grant receives one million dollars, to be spent on research of the recipient's choice." Management turned over a page of the flipchart. "The Niebnitz Grant is awarded for scientific sensibility." He wrote *science* on the flipchart. "Divergent thinking." He wrote *thought.* "And circumstantial predisposition to significant scientific breakthrough." He added *breakthrough* and then tapped all three words with his pointer. "Science. Thought. Breakthrough."

"What does this have to do with us?" Bennett whispered.

"Two years ago the Institut de Paris won a Niebnitz Grant," Management said.

"No, it didn't," I whispered. "A scientist *working* at the Institut won it."

"And *they* were using old-fashioned management techniques," Management said.

"Oh, no," I murmured. "Management expects us to win a Niebnitz Grant."

"How can they?" Bennett whispered. "Nobody even knows how they're awarded."

Management cast a cold eye in our direction. "The Niebnitz Grant Committee is looking for outstanding creative projects with the potential for significant scientific breakthroughs, which is what GRIM is all about. Now I'd like you to get in groups and write down five things you can do to win the Niebnitz Grant."

"Pray," Bennett said.

I grabbed a piece of paper and wrote down:

1. Optimize potential.
2. Facilitate empowerment.
3. Implement visioning.
4. Strategize priorities.
5. Augment core structures.

"What *is* that?" Bennett said, looking at the list. "Those make no sense."

"Neither does expecting us to win the Niebnitz Grant." I handed it in.

"Now let's get busy. You've got divergent thinking to do. Let's see some significant scientific breakthroughs."

Management marched out, his baton under his arm, but everyone just sat there, stunned, except Alicia Turnbull, who started taking rapid notes in her daybook, and Flip, who strolled in and started passing out pieces of paper.

"Projected Results: Significant Scientific Breakthrough," I said, shaking my head. "Well, bobbed hair certainly isn't it."

"Don't they know science doesn't work like that? You can't just order scientific breakthroughs. They happen when you look at something you've been working on for years and suddenly see a connection you never noticed before, or when you're looking for something else altogether. Sometimes they even happen by accident. Don't they know you can't get a scientific breakthrough just because you want one?"

"These are the people who gave Flip a promotion, remember?" I frowned. "What *is* 'circumstantial predisposition to significant scientific breakthrough'?"

"For Fleming it was looking at a contaminated culture and noticing the mold had killed the bacteria," Ben said.

"And how does Management know the Niebnitz Grant Committee gives the grant for creative projects with potential? How do they know there's a committee? For all we know, Niebnitz may be some old rich guy who gives money to projects that don't show any potential at all."

"In which case we're a shoo-in," Bennett said.

"For all we know, Niebnitz may give the grant to people whose names begin with *C*, or draw the names out of a hat."

Flip slouched over and handed one of her papers to Bennett. "Is this the memo explaining the simplified funding form?" he asked.

"No-*o-o-o*," she said, rolling her eyes. "It's a petition. To make the cafeteria a one hundred percent smoke-free environment." She sauntered away.

"I know what the *i* stands for," I said. *"Irritating."*

He shook his head. *"Insufferable."*

coonskin caps (may 1955—december 1955)——Children's fad inspired by the Walt Disney television series *Davy Crockett*, about the Kentucky frontier hero who fought at the Alamo and "kilt a bar" at age three. Part of a larger merchandising fad that included bow-and-arrow sets, toy knives, toy rifles, fringed shirts, powder horns, lunchboxes, jigsaw puzzles, coloring books, pajamas, panties, and seventeen recorded versions of "The Ballad of Davy Crockett," to which every child in America knew all the verses. As a result of the fad, a shortage of coonskins developed, and an earlier fad, the raccoon coat of the twenties, was ripped up to make caps. Some boys even got their hair cut in the shape of a coonskin cap. The fad collapsed right before Christmas of 1955, leaving merchandisers with hundreds of unwanted caps.

It occurred to me the next day while ransacking my lab for the clippings I'd given Flip to copy that Bennett's remark about having already met her new assistant must mean she'd been assigned to Bio. But in the afternoon Gina, looking hunted, came in to say, "I don't care what they say. I did the right thing hiring her. Shirl just printed out and collated twenty copies of an article I wrote. Correctly. I don't care if I am breathing in second-secondhand smoke.

"Second-secondhand smoke?"

"That's what Flip calls the air smokers breathe out. But I don't care. It's worth it."

"Shirl's been assigned to you?" I said.

She nodded. "This morning she delivered my mail. *My* mail. You should get her assigned to you."

"I will," I said, but that was easier said than done. Now that Flip had an assistant, she (and my clippings) had disappeared off the face of the earth. I searched the entire building twice, including the cafeteria, where large NO SMOKING signs had been put on all the tables, and Supply, where Desiderata was trying to figure out what printer cartridges were, and found Flip finally in my lab, sitting at my computer and typing something in.

She deleted it before I could see what it was and leaped up. If she'd been capable of it, I would have said she looked guilty.

"*You* weren't using it," she said. "You weren't even *here*."

"Did you make copies of those clippings I gave you Monday?" I said.

She looked blank.

"There was a copy of the personal ads on top of them."

She tossed her swag of hair. "Would you use the word *elegant* to describe me?"

She had added a hair wrap to her hank, a long thin strand of hair bound in bilious blue embroidery thread, and a band of duct tape across her forehead cut out to frame the *i*.

"No," I said.

"Well, nobody expects you to be all of them," she said, apropos of nothing. "Anyway, I don't know why you're so hooked on the personals. You've got that cowboy guy."

"What?"

"Billy Boy Somebody," she said, waving her hand at the phone. "He called and said he's in town for some seminar and you're supposed to meet him for dinner someplace. Tonight, I think. At the Nebraska Daisy or something. At seven o'clock."

I went over to my phone message pad. It was blank. "Didn't you write the message down?"

She sighed. "I can't do *everything*. That's why I was supposed to get an assistant, remember? So I wouldn't have to work so hard, only since she's a *smoker*, half the people I assigned her to don't want her in their labs, so I still have to copy all this stuff and go all the way down to Bio and stuff. I think smokers should be *forced* to give up cigarettes."

"Who all did you assign to her?"

"Bio and Product Development and Chem and Physics and Personnel and Payroll, and all the people who yell at me and make me do a lot of stuff. Or put in a camp or something where they couldn't expose the rest of us to all that smoke."

"Why don't you assign her to me? I don't mind that she smokes."

She put her hands on the hips of her blue leather skirt. "It causes cancer, you know," she said disapprovingly. "Besides, I'd never assign her to *you*. You're the only one who's halfway *nice* to me around here."

angel food cake (1880–90)

Food fad named to suggest the heavenly lightness and whiteness of the cake. Originated either at a restaurant in St. Louis, along the Hudson River, or in India. The secret of the cake was a dozen (or eleven, or fifteen) egg whites beaten into stiff glossy peaks. Difficult to bake, it inspired an entire folklore: The pan had to be ungreased, and no one could walk across the kitchen floor while it was baking. Supplanted by, of course, devil's food cake.

It was the Kansas Rose at five-thirty. "You got my message okay," Billy Ray said, coming out to meet me in the parking lot. He was wearing black jeans, a black-and-white cowboy shirt, and a white Stetson. His hair was longer than the last time I'd seen him. Long hair must be coming back in.

"Sort of," I said. "I'm here."

"Sorry it had to be so early," he said. "There's an evening workshop on 'Irrigation on the Internet' I don't want to miss." He took my arm. "This is supposed to be the trendiest place in town."

He was right. There was a half-hour wait, even with reservations, and every woman in line was wearing po-mo pink.

"Did you get your Targhees?" I asked him, leaning back against an ABSOLUTELY NO SMOKING sign.

"Yep, and they're great. Low maintenance, high tolerance for cold, and fifteen pounds of wool in a season."

"Wool?" I said. "I thought Targhees were cows."

"Nobody's raising cows anymore," he said, frowning as if I should know that. "The whole cholesterol thing. Lamb's got a lower cholesterol count, and shearling's supposed to be the hot new fashion fabric for winter."

"Bobby Jay," the hostess, who was wearing a red gingham pinafore and hair wraps, called out.

"That's us," I said.

"We don't want to sit anywhere close to where the smoking section used to be," Billy Ray said, and we followed her to the table.

The sunflower fad had apparently come here to die. They were entwined in the white picket fence around our table, framed on the wall, painted on the bathroom doors, embroidered on the napkins. A large artificial bunch was stuck in a Mason jar in the middle of our sunflowered tablecloth.

"Cool, huh?" Billy Ray said, opening his sunflower-shaped menu. "Everybody says prairie's going to be the next big fad."

"I thought shearling was," I muttered, picking up the menu. Prairie cuisine wasn't so much hot as substantial—chicken-fried steak, cream gravy, corn on the cob, all served family-style.

"Something to drink?" a waiter in buckskin and a knotted sunflower bandanna asked.

I looked at the menu. They had espresso, cappuccino, and caffè latte, also very big in prairie days. No iced tea.

"Iced tea's the Kansas state beverage," I told the waiter. "How can you not have it?"

He'd apparently been taking lessons from Flip. He rolled his eyes, sighed expertly, and said, "Iced tea is outré."

A word never uttered on the prairie, I thought, but Billy Ray was already ordering meat loaf, mashed potatoes, and cappuccino for both of us.

"So, tell me about this thing you're researching that's got you working weekends."

I did. "The problem is I've got causes coming out my ears," I said, after I'd explained what I'd been doing. "Female equality, bicycling, a French fashion designer named Poiret, World War One, and Coco Chanel, who singed her hair off when a heater exploded. Unfortunately, none of them seems to be the main source."

Our dinner arrived, on brown earthenware platters decorated with sunflowers. The coleslaw was garnished with fresh basil, which I didn't remember as being big on the prairie either, and the meat loaf was garnished with lemon slices.

Billy Ray told me about the merits of sheep-raising while we ate. Sheep were healthy, profitable, no trouble to herd, and you could graze them anywhere, all of which I would have been more inclined to believe if he hadn't told me the same thing about raising longhorns six months ago.

"Dessert?" the waiter said, and brought over the pastry cart.

I figured a prairie dessert would probably be gooseberry pie or maybe canned peaches, but it was the usual suspects: crème brûlée, tiramisu, "and our newest dessert, bread pudding."

Well, that sounded like a Kansas dessert, all right, the sort of thing you were reduced to eating after the cow died and the grasshoppers ate up the crops.

"I'll have the tiramisu," I said.

"Me too," Billy Ray said. "I've always hated bread pudding. It's like eating leftovers."

"Everybody *raves* about our bread pudding," the waiter said reproachfully. "It's our most popular dessert."

The bad thing about studying trends is that you can't ever turn it off. You sit there across from your date eating tiramisu, and instead of thinking what a nice guy he is, you find yourself thinking about trends in desserts and how they always seem to be gooey and calorie-laden in direct proportion to the obsession with dieting.

Take tiramisu, which has chocolate and whipped cream and two kinds of cheese. And burnt-sugar cake, which was big in the forties, in spite of wartime rationing.

Pineapple upside-down cake was a fad in the twenties, a dessert I hope doesn't make a comeback anytime soon; chiffon cake in the fifties; chocolate fondue in the sixties.

I wondered if Bennett was immune to food trends, too, and what his ideas on bread pudding and chocolate cheesecake were.

"You thinking about hair-bobbing again?" Billy Ray said. "Maybe you're looking at too many things. This conference I'm at says you've got to niff."

"Niff?"

"NYF. Narrow Your Focus. Eliminate all the peripherals and focus in on the core variables. This hair-bobbing thing can only have one cause, right? You've got to narrow your focus to the likeliest possibilities and concentrate on those. It works, too. I tried it on a case of sheep mange. You're sure you won't come to my workshop with me?"

"I have to go to the library," I said.

"You should get the book. *Five Steps to Focusing on Success.*"

After dinner Billy Ray went off to niff, and I went over to the library to see about Browning. Lorraine wasn't there. A girl wearing duct tape, hair wraps, and a sullen expression was. "It's three weeks overdue," she said.

"That's impossible," I said. "I only checked it out last week. And I checked it in. On Monday." After I'd tried Pippa on Flip and decided Browning didn't know what he was talking about. I'd checked in Browning and checked out *Othello*, that other story about undue influences.

She sighed. "Our computer shows it as still checked out. Have you looked around at home?"

"Is Lorraine here?" I asked.

She rolled her eyes. "No-o-o-o."

I decided it was the better part of valor to wait until she was and went over to the stacks to look for Browning myself. *The Complete Works* wasn't there, and I couldn't remember the name of the book Billy Ray had suggested. I pulled out two books by Willa Cather, who knew what prairie cooking had actually been like, and *Far from the Madding Crowd*, which I remembered as having sheep in it, and then wandered around, trying to remember the name of Billy Ray's book and hoping for inspiration.

Libraries have been responsible for a lot of significant scientific breakthroughs. Darwin was reading Malthus for recreation (which should tell you something about Darwin), and Alfred Wegener was wandering around the Marburg University library, idly spinning the globe and browsing through scientific papers, when he got the idea of continental drift. But nothing came to me, not even the name of Billy Ray's book. I went over to the business section to see if I would remember the name of the book when I saw it.

Something about narrowing the focus, eliminating all the peripherals. "It can only have one cause, right?" Billy Ray had said.

Wrong. In a linear system it might, but hair-bobbing wasn't like sheep mange. It was like one of Bennett's chaotic systems. There were dozens of variables, and all of them were important. They fed into each other, iterating and reiterating, crossing and colliding, affecting each other in ways no one would expect. Maybe the problem wasn't that I had too many causes, but that I didn't have enough. I went over to the nine hundreds and checked out *Those Crazy Twenties; Flappers, Flivvers, and Flagpole-Sitters;* and *The 1920's: A Sociological Study,* and as many other books on the twenties as I could carry, and took them up to the desk.

"I show an overdue book for you," the girl said. "It's four weeks overdue."

I went home, excited for the first time that I was on the right track, and started work on the new variables.

The twenties had been awash in fads: jazz, hip flasks, rolled-down stockings, dance crazes, raccoon coats, mah-jongg, running marathons, dance marathons, kissing marathons, Stutz Bearcats, flagpole-sitting, tree-sitting, crossword puzzles. And somewhere in all those rouged knees and rain slickers and rocking-chair derbies was the trigger that had set off the hair-bobbing craze.

I worked until very late and then went to bed with *Far from the Madding Crowd.* I was right. It was about sheep. And fads. In Chapter Five one of the sheep fell over a cliff, and the others followed, plummeting one after the other onto the rocks below.

3. tributaries

"Please your honors," said he, "I'm able,
By means of a secret charm, to draw
All creatures living beneath the sun,
That creep or fly or run,
After me so as you never saw!"

robert browning

diorama wigs (1750—60)——Hair fad of the court of Louis XVI inspired by Madame de Pompadour, who was fond of dressing her hair in unusual ways. Hair was draped over a frame stuffed with cotton wool or straw and cemented with a paste that hardened, and the hair was powdered and decorated with pearls and flowers. The fad rapidly got out of hand. Frames grew as high as three feet tall, and the decorations became elaborate and then pictorial. Hairdos had waterfalls, cupids, and scenes from novels. Naval battles, complete with ships and smoke, were waged on top of women's heads, and one widow, overcome with mourning for her dead husband, had his tombstone erected in her hair. Died out with the advent of the French Revolution and the resultant shortage of heads to put wigs on.

Rivers are not just wide streams. They are drainage basins for dozens, sometimes hundreds of tributaries. The Lena River in Siberia, for example, drains an area of over a million square miles, including the Karenga, the Olekma, the Vitim, and the Aldan rivers, and a thousand smaller streams and brooks, some of which follow such distant, convoluted courses it would never occur to you they connected to the Lena, thousands of miles away.

The events leading up to a scientific breakthrough are frequently not only random but far afield from science. Take the measles. Einstein had them when he was four and his father was only trying to amuse a sick little boy when he gave him a pocket compass to play with. And the keys to the universe.

Fleming's life is a whole system of coincidences, beginning with his father, who was a groundskeeper on the Churchill estate. When ten-year-old Winston fell in the lake, Fleming's father jumped in and rescued him. The grateful family rewarded him by sending his son Alexander to medical school.

Take Penzias and Wilson. Robert Dicke, at Princeton University, talked to P.J.E. Peebles about calculating how hot the Big Bang was. He did, realized it was hot enough to be detectable as a residue of radiation, and told Peter G. Roll and David T. Wilkinson that they should look for microwaves.

Peebles (are you following this?) gave a talk at Johns Hopkins in which he mentioned Roll and Wilkinson's project. Ken Turner of the Carnegie Institute heard the lecture and mentioned it to Bernard Burke at MIT, a friend of Penzias. (Still with me?)

When Penzias called Burke on something else altogether (his daughter's birthday party probably), he told Burke about their impossible background noise. And Burke told him to call Wilkinson and Roll.

During the next week several things happened:

I fed flagpole-sitting and mah-jongg data into the computer, Management declared HiTek a smoke-free building, Gina's daughter, Brittany, turned five, and Dr. Turnbull, of all people, came to see me.

She was wearing a po-mo pink silk campshirt and pink jeans and a friendly smile. The jeans and camp shirt meant she was following HiTek's dressing-down edict. I had no idea what the smile meant.

"Dr. Foster," she said, turning it on me full force, "just the person I wanted to see."

"If you're looking for a package, Dr. Turnbull," I said warily, "Flip hasn't been here yet."

She laughed, a merry, tinkling laugh I wouldn't have thought she was capable of. "Call me Alicia," she said. "No package. I just thought I'd drop by and chat with you. You know, so we could get to know each other better. We've really only talked a couple of times."

Once, I thought, and you yelled at me. What are you really here for?

"So," she said, sitting on one of the lab tables and crossing her legs. "Where did you go to school?"

"Getting to know you" at HiTek usually consists of "So, are you dating anybody?" or, in the case of Elaine, "Are you into high-impact aerobics?" but maybe this was Alicia's idea of small talk. "I got my doctorate at Baylor."

She smiled yet more brightly. "It was in sociology, wasn't it?"

"And stats," I said.

"A double major," she said approvingly. "Was that where you did your undergrad work?"

She couldn't be an industry spy. We worked for the same industry. And all this was up in Personnel's records anyway. "No," I said. "Where'd you do your graduate work?"

End of conversation. "Indiana," she said, as if I'd asked for something that was none of my business, and slid her pink rear off the table, but she didn't leave. She stood looking around the lab at the piles of data.

"You have so much stuff in here," she said, examining one of the untidy piles.

Maybe Management had sent her to spy on Workplace Organization. "I plan to get things straightened up as soon as I finish my funding forms," I said.

She wandered over to look at the flagpole-sitting piles. "I've already turned mine in."

Of course.

"And messiness is good. Susan Holyrood and Dan Twofeathers's labs were both messy. R. C. Mendez says it's a creativity indicator."

I had no idea who any of these people were or what was going on here. Something, obviously. Maybe Management had sent her to look for signs of smoking. Alicia had forgotten all about the friendly smile and was circling the lab like a shark.

"Bennett told me you're working on fads source analysis. Why did you decide to work with fads?"

"Everybody else was doing it."

"Really?" she said eagerly. "Who are the other scientists?"

"That was a joke," I said lamely, and set about the hopeless task of trying to explain it. "You know, fads, something people do just because everybody else is doing it?"

"Oh, I get it," she said, which meant she didn't, but she seemed more bemused than offended. "Wittiness can be a creativity indicator, too, can't it? What do *you* think the most important quality for a scientist is?"

"Luck," I said.

Now she did look offended. *"Luck?"*

"And good assistants," I said. "Look at Roy Plunkett. His assistant's using a silver gasket on the tank of chlorofluorocarbons was what led to the discovery of Teflon. Or Becquerel. He had the good luck to hire a young Polish girl to help him with his radiation therapy. Her name was Marie Curie."

"That's very interesting," she said. "Where did you say you did your undergrad work?"

"University of Oregon," I said.

"How old were you when you got your doctorate?"

We were back to the third degree. "Twenty-six."

"How old are you now?"

"Thirty-one," I said, and that was apparently the right answer because she turned the brights back on. "Did you grow up in Oregon?"

"No," I said. "Nebraska."

This, on the other hand, was *not*. Alicia switched off the smile, said, "I have a lot of work to do," and left without a backward glance. Whatever she'd wanted, apparently witty and messy weren't enough.

I sat there staring at the screen wondering what that had been all about, and Flip came in wearing an assortment of duct tape and a pair of backless clogs.

She should have used some of the duct tape on the clogs. They slopped off her feet with every step, and she had to half-shuffle her way down the hall to me. The clogs and the duct tape were both the bilious electric blue she'd worn the other day.

"What do you call that color?" I asked.

"Cerenkhov blue."

Of course. After the bluish radiation in nuclear reactors. How appropriate. In fairness, though, I had to admit it wasn't the first time a faddish color had been given a wretched name. Back in Louis XVI's day, color names had been downright nauseating. Sewerage, arsenic, smallpox, and Sick Spaniard had all been hit names for yellow-green.

Flip handed me a piece of paper. "You need to sign this," she said.

It was a petition to declare the staff lounge a nonsmoking

area. "Where will people be allowed to smoke if they can't smoke in the lounge?" I said.

"They shouldn't smoke. It causes cancer," she said righteously. "I think people who smoke shouldn't be allowed to have jobs." She tossed her hank of hair. "And they should have to live someplace where their secondhand smoke can't hurt the rest of us."

"Really, Herr Goebbels," I said, forgetting that ignorance is the biggest trend of all, and handed the petition back to her.

"Second-secondhand smoke is dangerous," she said huffily.

"So is meanness." I turned back to the computer.

"How much does a crown cost?" she said.

It seemed to be my day for questions out of left field. "A crown?" I said, bewildered. "You mean, like a tiara?"

"No-o-o," she said. "A *crown.*"

I tried to picture a crown on top of Flip's hank of hair, with her hair wrap hanging down one side, and failed. But whatever she was talking about, I'd better pay attention because it was likely to be the next big fad. Flip might be incompetent, insubordinate, and generally insufferable, but she was right there on the cutting edge of fashion.

"A crown," I said. "Made out of gold?" I pantomimed placing one on my head. "With points?"

"Points?" she said, outraged. "It better not have points. A *crown.*"

"I'm sorry, Flip," I said. "I don't know—"

"You're a *sci*entist," she said. "You're supposed to know scientific terms," she said.

I wondered if *crown* had become a scientific term the way duct tape had become a personal errand.

"A *crown!*" she said, sighed enormously, and clopped out of the lab and down the hall.

It was my day for encounters I couldn't make heads or tails of, and that included my hair-bobbing data. I was sorry I'd ever gotten the idea of including the other fads of the day. There were way too many of them, and none of them made any sense.

Peanut-pushing, for instance, and flagpole-sitting, and painting knees with rouge. College kids had painted old Model T's with clever slogans like "Banana oil" and "Oh, you kid!", middle-aged housewives had dressed up like Chinese maidens and played mah-jongg, and fads had seemed to come out of the woodwork, superseding each other in months and sometimes weeks. The black bottom replaced mah-jongg, which had replaced King Tut, and the whole thing was so chaotic it was impossible to sort out.

Crossword puzzles were the only fad that was halfway reasonable, and even that was a puzzle. The fad had started in the fall of 1924, well after hair-bobbing, but crossword puzzles had been around since the 1800s, and the *New York World* had published a weekly crossword since 1913.

And reasonable, on closer examination, wasn't really the word. A minister had passed out crosswords during church that, on being solved, revealed the scripture lesson. Women had worn dresses decorated with black-and-white squares, and hats and stockings to match, and Broadway put on a revue called "Puzzles of 1925." People had cited crosswords as the cause of their divorces, secretaries wore pocket dictionaries around their wrists like bracelets, doctors warned of eyestrain, and in Budapest a writer left a suicide note in the form of a crossword puzzle, a puzzle, by the way, which the police never solved, probably because they were already consumed with the next fad: the Charleston.

Bennett stuck his head in the door. "Have you got a minute? I need to ask you a question." He came in. He had

changed his checked shirt for a faded plaid one that was neither madras nor Ivy League, and he was carrying a copy of the
simplified funding form.

"A two-letter word for an Egyptian sun god?" I said. "It's
Ra."

He grinned. "No, I was just wondering if Flip had
brought you a copy of the memo Management said they'd
send around. Explaining the simplified funding form?"

"Yes and no," I said. "I had to get one from Gina." I
fished it out from a pile of twenties books.

"Great," he said, "I'll go make a copy and bring this
back."

"That's okay," I said. "You can keep it."

"You finished filling out your funding forms?"

"No," I said. "Read the memo."

He looked at it. " 'Page nineteen, Question forty-four-C.
To find the primary extensional funding formula, multiply the
departmental needs analysis by the fiscal base quotient, unless
the project involves calibrated structuring, in which case the
quotient should be calculated according to Section W-A of
the accompanying instructions." He turned the paper over.
"Where are the accompanying instructions?"

"No one knows," I said.

He handed the memo back to me. "Maybe I don't have to
go to France to study chaos. Maybe I could study it right
here," he said, shaking his head. "Thanks," and he started to
leave.

"Speaking of which," I said, "how's your information diffusion project coming?"

"The lab's all ready," he said. "I can get the macaques as
soon as I finish this stupid funding form, which should be in
about"—he pulled a calculator out of his threadbare pants and
punched in numbers—"six thousand years from now."

Flip slouched in and handed us each a stapled stack of papers.

"What's this?" Bennett said. "The accompanying instructions?"

"No-o-o," Flip said, tossing her head. "It's the FDA report on the health hazards of smoking."

dance marathon (1923—33) —— Endurance fad in which the object was to dance the longest to earn money. Couples pinched and kicked each other to stay awake, and when that failed, took turns sleeping on their partner's shoulder for as long as 150 days. The marathons became a gruesome spectator sport, with people watching to see who would have hallucinations brought on by sleep deprivation, collapse, or, in the case of Homer Moorhouse, drop dead, and the New Jersey SPCA complained that the marathons were cruel to (human) animals. Persisted into the first years of the Depression simply because people needed the money, which worked out to a little over a penny an hour. If you won.

Tuesday I met the new assistant interdepartmental communications liaison. I'd decided I couldn't wait any longer for the accompanying instructions and was working on the funding forms when I noticed that the bottom of page 28 read, "List all," and the top of the next page read, "to the diversification quotient." I looked at the page number. It read "42."

I went down to see if Gina had the missing pages. She was sitting in a tangle of sacks, wrapping paper, and ribbons. "You *are* coming to Brittany's party, aren't you?" she said. "You have to come. There are going to be six five-year-olds and six mothers, and I don't know which is worse."

"I'll be there," I promised, and asked her about the missing pages.

"There are missing *pages*?" she said. "My funding form's at home. When am I going to be able to fill out missing pages? I've still got to go buy plates and cups and decorations *and* fix the refreshments."

I escaped and went back to the lab. A gray-haired woman was sitting at the computer, rapidly typing in numbers.

"Sorry," she said as soon as I came in the room. "Flip said I could use your computer, but I don't want to get in your way." She began rapidly touching keys to save the file.

"Are you Flip's new assistant?" I asked, looking at her curiously. She was thin, with tan, leathery skin, like Billy Ray would have after another thirty years of riding the range.

"Shirl Creets," she said, shaking my hand. She had a grip like Billy Ray's, and her fingers were stained a yellowish brown, which explained how Sarah and Elaine had known she was a smoker "just by looking at her."

"Flip was using Dr. Turnbull's computer," she said, and her voice was hoarse, too, "and she told me to come up here and use yours, that you wouldn't mind. I'll be off this as soon as I save the file. I haven't been smoking," she added.

"You can smoke if you want," I said. "And you can use the computer. I've got to go over to Personnel anyway and pick up a different funding allocation form. This one's missing pages."

"I'll go get it for you," Shirl said, getting up immediately and taking the form from me. "Which pages is it missing?"

"Twenty-nine through forty-one," I said, "and maybe some at the end, I don't know. Mine only goes up to page sixty-eight. But you don't have to—"

"What are assistants *for*? Do you want me to make an extra copy so you can do a rough draft?"

"That would be nice, thank you," I said, in shock, and sat down at the computer.

I had been nice to Flip, and look what it had gotten me. I took it back that Browning knew anything about trends, Pied Piper or no Pied Piper.

The data Shirl had been typing in were still there. It was some kind of table. "Carbanks—48, Twofeathers—34," it read. "Holyrood—61, Chin—39." I wondered what project Alicia was working on now.

Shirl was back in five minutes flat, with a stack of neatly collated and stapled sheafs. "I put copies of the missing pages in your original, and made you two extra copies just in case." She set them gently down on the lab table and handed me another thick sheaf. "While I was in the copy room, I found these clippings. Flip didn't know who they belonged to. I thought they might be yours."

She held up a stack of clippings on dance marathons, neatly paper-clipped to a set of copies.

"I assumed you wanted copies," she said.

"Thank you," I said, astounded. "I don't suppose you could talk Flip into assigning you to me?"

"I doubt it," she said. "She seems to like you." She set the clippings on the lab table and began straightening the top of it. She fished the chaos theory book out of the mess.

"Mandelbrot diagrams," she said interestedly. "Is that what you're researching?"

"No," I said. "Fad origins. I was just reading that out of curiosity. They are connected, though. Fads are a facet of the chaotic system of society, with a number of variables contributing to them."

She stacked *Brave New World* and *All's Well that Ends Well* on top of the chaos theory book without comment and picked up *Flappers, Flivvers, and Flagpole-Sitters.* "What made you choose fads?" she said disapprovingly.

"You don't like fads?"

"I just think there are more direct ways of influencing society than starting a fad. I had a physics teacher who used to say, 'Pay no attention to what other people are doing. Do what you want, and you can change the world.'"

"Oh, I don't want to discover how to start them," I said. "I suppose HiTek does, and that's why they keep funding the project, although if the mechanism is as complex as it's beginning to look, they'll never be able to isolate the critical variable, at which point they'll probably stop funding me." I looked at the dance marathon notes. "What *I* want to do is understand what causes them."

"Why?" she said curiously.

"Because I just want to understand. Why do people act the way they do? Why do they all suddenly decide to play the same game or wear the same clothes or believe the same thing? In the 1920s smoking was a fad. Now it's *anti*smoking. Why? Is it instinctive behavior or societal influences? Or something in the air? The Salem witch trials were caused by fear and greed, but they're always around, and we don't burn witches all the time, so there must be something else going on.

"I just don't understand what," I said. "And it doesn't look like I will anytime soon. I don't seem to be getting anywhere. *You* don't happen to know what caused hair-bobbing, do you?"

"It's going slowly?" she said.

"Slow isn't the word," I said. I gestured with the marathon dancing copies. "I feel like *I'm* in a dance marathon contest. Most of the time it's not dancing at all, it's just putting one foot in front of the other, trying to hang on and stay awake. Trying to remember why you signed up in the first place."

"My physics teacher used to say that science was one percent inspiration and ninety-nine percent perspiration," she said.

"And fifty percent filling out nonsimplified funding forms," I said. I picked up one of the extra copies. "I'd better take one of these over to Gina."

"I've already taken one to Dr. Damati," she said. "Oh, and I need to get back there. I promised her I'd wrap Brittany's presents for her."

"You're *sure* you can't persuade Flip?" I said.

After she left, I started work on page 29, but it didn't make any more sense than when it had been missing, and I was starting to feel vaguely itch again. I took one of the extra copies and went down to Bio to Bennett's lab.

Alicia was there, head to head with Bennett at the computer, but he looked up immediately and smiled at me.

"Hi," he said. "Come on in."

"No, that's okay. I didn't mean to interrupt," I said, smiling at Alicia. She didn't smile back. "I just wanted to bring you a complete funding form." I handed him the funding form. "There were pages missing in the ones Flip passed out."

"Incompetent," he said. "Incorrigible. Incapacitating."

Alicia was actively glaring at me.

"Intruding," I said. "Which is what I'm doing on your meeting. I'll talk to you later." I headed for the door.

"No, wait," he said. "You'll be interested in this. Dr. Turnbull was just telling me about her project." He looked at Alicia. "Tell Dr. Foster what you've been doing."

"I've taken the data on all the previous Niebnitz Grant winners: scientific discipline, project area, educational background—"

That explained the third degree I'd gotten from her yesterday. She had been trying to determine if I fit the profile, and from the look she was giving me, I must not have even placed.

"—age, gender, ethnic group, political affiliation." She scrolled through several screens, and I recognized a chart like the one Shirl had just been working on. "I'm running regressions to determine the relevant characteristics and then analyzing those to construct a profile of the typical Niebnitz Grant recipient and the criteria the Niebnitz Grant Committee uses to make their choices."

The committee's criteria were originality of thought and creativity, I thought. Assuming there *is* a committee.

"I haven't completed the regressions yet, but some patterns are emerging." She called up a spreadsheet. "The grant is given at a median interval of one point nine years apart, but the closest two grants have ever been given is one point two years, which means the grant won't be given until May at the earliest."

It didn't mean any such thing, and I would have said so, but she was into it now.

"Distribution of the awards follows a cyclical pattern, with academic institutions, research labs, and commercial corporations alternating, the next one being a corporation, which gives us an advantage, *and*"—she switched to a different spreadsheet—"there is a definite bias toward scientists west of the Mississippi, which is also an advantage, *and* a bias toward the biological sciences. I haven't determined the specific area yet, but I should have that part of the profile by tomorrow."

All of which sounded suspiciously like science on demand. I looked at Bennett to see what he thought about all this, but he was watching the screen intently, abstractedly, as if he'd forgotten we were there.

Well, of course he was interested. Why wouldn't he be? If he could win the Niebnitz Grant, he could go back to the Loue River to work on chaos theory and forget all about forms and Flip and the uncertainties of funding.

Except science doesn't work like that. You can't handicap significant breakthroughs like they were a horse race.

But this wouldn't be the first time somebody'd convinced himself of something that wasn't true where money was involved. Take the stock market fad of the late twenties. Or the Dutch tulip craze of the 1600s. In 1634, the prices of tulips that were fancier or prettier or rarer than others started going up, and suddenly everybody—merchants, princes, peasants, brothers, sisters, husbands, wives—was buying and selling bulbs like mad. Prices skyrocketed, speculators made fortunes overnight, and people hocked their wooden shoes *and* the dike to buy a bulb that might cost as much as twelve annual incomes. And then for no reason, the market collapsed, and it was just like October 29, 1929, only with no skyscraper windows for Dutch stockholders to fling themselves out of.

Not to mention chain letters, pyramid schemes, and the Florida land boom.

"The other factor that needs to be considered is the name of the grant," Alicia was saying. "Niebnitz may refer either to Ludwig Niebnitz, who was an obscure eighteenth-century botanist, or to Karl Niebnitz von Drull, who lived in fifteenth-century Bavaria. If it's Ludwig, that would account for the biological bias. Von Drull was more famous. His area was alchemy."

"I have to go," I said, standing up. "If I'm going to switch my fads project to changing lead into gold, I'll need to get busy," and I walked out.

Bennett followed me out into the hall. "Thanks for bringing the funding form."

"We have to stick together against the forces of Flip," I said. "Have you met her new assistant?"

"Yeah, she's great," he said. "I wonder whatever possessed her to take a job like this?"

"NIEBNITZ may also be an acronym," Alicia said from the doorway. "In which case—"

I took my leave and went back up to my lab.

Flip was there, typing something on my computer. "How would you describe me?" she asked.

I looked around the lab. It was spotless. Shirl had cleaned off the lab tables and put all my clippings in folders. In alphabetical order.

Inescapable, I thought. Impacted. "Inextricable," I said.

"That sounds good," she said. "Does it have two *k*s or one?"

dr. spock (1945–65)——— Child care fad, inspired by the pediatrician's book, *Baby and Child Care*, growing interest in psychology, and the fragmentation of the extended family. Spock advocated a more permissive approach than previous child care books and advised flexibility in feeding schedules and attention to child development, advice which far too many parents misinterpreted as letting the child do whatever it wanted. Died out when the first generation of Dr. Spock–raised children became teenagers, grew their hair down to their shoulders, and began blowing up administration buildings.

Wednesday I went to the birthday party. I'd arranged to leave early and was putting on my coat when Flip slouched in, wearing a laced bodice and duct-tape-decorated jeans, and handed me a piece of paper.

"I don't have time for any petitions," I said.

"It's not a petition," she said, tossing her hair. "It's a memo about the funding forms."

The memo said the funding forms were due on the twenty-third, which I already knew.

"You're supposed to turn the form in to me."

I nodded and handed it back to her. "Take this down to Dr. O'Reilly's lab," I said, pulling on my gloves.

She sighed. "He's never there. He's always in Dr. Turnbull's lab."

"Then take it to Dr. Turnbull's lab."

"They're always together. He's com*plete*ly raved about her, you know."

No, I thought, I didn't know that.

"They're always sitting at the computer together. I don't know what she sees in him. He's com*plete*ly swarb," Flip said, picking at the duct tape on the back of her hand. "Maybe she can make him not so fashion-impaired."

And if she does, I thought irritatedly, there goes his nonfadness, and I'll never figure out why he was immune to them.

"What does *sophisticated* mean?" Flip asked.

"Cosmopolitan," I said, "but you're not," and left for the party. The weather had turned colder. We usually get one big snowstorm in October, and it looked like the weather was gearing up for it.

Gina was nearly hysterical by the time I got there. "You won't believe what Brittany decided she wanted after I said she couldn't have Barney," she said, pointing to the decorations, which were a pink that bore no relation to postmodern.

"Barbie!" Brittany shouted. She was wearing a Little Mermaid dress and bright pink hair wraps. "Did you bring me a present?"

The other little girls were all wearing Pocahontas pinafores except for a sweet little blonde named Peyton, who was wearing a Lion King jumper and light-up sneakers.

"Are you married?" Peyton's mother said to me.

"No," I said.

She shook her head. "So many guys have intimacy issues these days. Peyton, we're not opening presents yet."

"Are you dating anyone?" Lindsay's mother said.

"We're going to open presents later, Brittany," Gina said. "First we're all going to play a game. Bethany, it's Brittany's birthday."

She attempted a game involving balloons with pink Barbies on them and then gave up and let Brittany open her presents.

"Open Sandy's first," Gina said, handing her the book. "No, Caitlin, these are Brittany's presents."

Brittany ripped the paper off *Toads and Diamonds* and looked at it blankly.

"That was my favorite fairy tale when I was little," I said. "It's about a girl who meets a good fairy, only she doesn't know it because the fairy's in disguise—" but Brittany had already tossed it aside and was ripping open a Barbie doll in a glittery dress.

"Totally Hair Barbie!" she shrieked.

"Mine," Peyton said, and made a grab that left Brittany holding nothing but Barbie's arm.

"She broke Totally Hair Barbie!" Brittany wailed.

Peyton's mother stood up and said calmly, "Peyton, I think you need a time-out."

I thought Peyton needed a good swat, or at least to have Totally Hair Barbie taken away from her and given back to Brittany, but instead her mother led her to the door of Gina's bedroom. "You can come out when you're in control of your feelings," she said to Peyton, who looked like she was in control to me.

"I can't believe you're still using time-outs," Chelsea's mother said. "Everybody's using holding now."

"Holding?" I asked.

"You hold the child immobile on your lap until the negative behavior stops. It produces a feeling of interceptive safety."

"Really," I said, looking toward the bedroom door. I would have hated trying to hold Peyton against her will.

"Holding's been totally abandoned," Lindsay's mother said. "We use EE."

"EE?" I said.

"Esteem Enhancement," Lindsay's mother said. "EE addresses the positive peripheral behavior no matter how negative the primary behavior is."

"Positive peripheral behavior?" Gina said dubiously.

"When Peyton took the Barbie away from Brittany just now," Lindsay's mother said, obviously delighted to explain, "you would have said, 'My, Peyton, what an assertive grip you have.' "

Brittany opened Swim 'n' Dive Barbie, Stick 'n' Peel Barbie, Barbie's City Nights cycle, and an elaborately coiffed and veiled Barbie in a wedding dress. "Romantic Bride Barbie," Brittany said, transported.

"Can we have cake now?" Lindsay said, and Peyton must have had her little ear to the door because she opened it, looking not particularly contrite, said, "I feel better about myself now," and climbed up to the table.

"No cake," Gina said. "Too much cholesterol. Frozen yogurt and Snapple," and all the little girls came running as if they'd heard the Pied Piper's flute.

The mothers and I picked up wrapping paper and ribbon, checking carefully for stray Barbie high heels and microscopic accessories. Danielle's mother smoothed down Romantic Bride Barbie's net overskirt. "I wonder if Lisa'd like a dress like this," she said. "She's trying to talk Eric into getting married sometime this summer."

"Are you going to be her matron of honor?" Chelsea's mother asked. "What colors is she going to have?"

"She hasn't decided. Black and white is really in, but she already did that the last time she got married."

"Postmodern pink," I said. "It's the new color for spring."

"I look washed out in pink," Danielle's mother said. "And she's still got to talk him into it. He says, why can't they just live together?"

Lindsay's mother picked up Romantic Bride Barbie and began fluffing up her bouffant sleeves. "I always said I'd never get married again, after that *jerk* Matt," she said. "But I don't know, lately I've been feeling sort of . . . I don't know . . ."

Itch? I thought.

The phone rang, and Gina went into the bedroom to get it, and everybody else adjourned to the kitchen.

There was a shriek from the kitchen, and everybody went in to enhance esteem. I picked up Romantic Bride Barbie and looked at the pink net rosebuds and white satin flounces, marveling. Barbie's a fad that should have lasted, at the most, for two seasons. Even the Shirley Temple doll had only been a fad for three.

Instead, Barbie's well into her thirties and more of a fad than ever, even in these days of feminism and non-gender-biased child-rearing. She'd be the perfect thing to study for what causes fads, but I wasn't sure I wanted to know. Barbie's one of those fads whose popularity makes you lose all faith in the human race.

Gina came out of the bedroom. "It's for you," she said, looking speculatively at me. "You can take it in the bedroom."

I put down Romantic Bride Barbie and stood up.

"It's *my* birthday!" Brittany shrieked.

"My, Peyton," Lindsay's mother said, "what a *creative* thing to do with your frozen yogurt."

Gina hurried into the kitchen, and I went into the bedroom.

It was done in violets, with a purple cordless phone. I picked it up.

"Howdy," Billy Ray said. "Guess where I'm calling from?"

"How did you find out I was here?"

"I called HiTek, and your assistant told me."

"*Flip* gave you the number?" I said. "Correctly?"

"I don't know what her name was. Raspy voice. Coughed a lot."

Shirl. She must be putting some more of Alicia's data on my computer.

"Well, so, listen, I'm on my way through the Rockies right now and—hang on. Tunnel coming up. Call you back as soon as I'm through it." There was a hum, and a click.

I hung up the phone and sat there on Gina's violet-covered bed, wondering how Billy Ray ever got any ranching done when he was never at the ranch, and pondering the appeal of Barbie.

Part of it must be that she's been able to incorporate other fads over the years. In the mid-sixties, Barbie had ironed hair and Carnaby Street clothes, in the seventies granny dresses, in the eighties leotards and leg warmers.

Nowadays there are astronaut Barbies and management Barbies, and even a doctor, though it's hard to imagine Barbie making it through junior high, let alone medical school.

Billy Ray had apparently forgotten all about me, and so had Peyton's mother. She opened the door, said, ". . . and I want you to stay in time-out until you've decided to relate to your peers," and ushered in a frozen yogurt-covered Peyton.

Neither of them saw me, especially not Peyton, who flung herself against the door, red-faced and whimpering, and then, when it was apparent that wasn't going to work, dropped to her hands and knees next to the bed and pulled out a tablet and crayons.

She sat down cross-legged in the middle of the floor,

opened the box of crayons, selected a pink one, and began to draw.

"Hi," I said, and was happy to see her jump a foot. "What are you doing?"

"You're not supposed to talk in a time-out," she said righteously.

You're not supposed to color either, I thought, wishing Billy Ray would remember he was calling me back.

She selected a green crayon and bent over the tablet, drawing earnestly. I moved the phone around to the other side of the bed so I could see the picture.

"What are you drawing?" I asked. "A butterfly?"

She rolled her eyes. "*No-o-o,*" she said. "It's a story."

"A story?" I said, tilting my head around to see it better. "About what?"

"About *Bar*bie." She sighed, a dead ringer for Flip, and chose a bright blue crayon.

Why do only the awful things become fads? I thought. Eye-rolling and Barbie and bread pudding. Why never chocolate cheesecake or thinking for yourself?

I looked more closely at the picture. It looked more like a Mandelbrot diagram than a story. It appeared to be some sort of map, or maybe a diagram, with many lines of tiny lavender stars and pink zigzag symbols intersecting across the paper. Peyton had obviously been working on it during a number of time-outs.

"What's this?" I said, pointing at a row of purple zigzags.

"See," she said, bringing the tablet and the crayons up onto my lap, "Barbie went to her Malibu Beach House." She drew a scalloped blue line above the zigzags. "It's very far. They had to go in her Jaguar."

"And that's this line?" I said, pointing at the blue scallops.

"No-o-o," she said, irritated at all these interruptions.

"That's to show what she was wearing. See, when she goes to the Malibu Beach House she wears her blue hat. So they all got to the Malibu Beach House," she said, walking her crayon like a doll across the paper, "and Barbie said, 'Let's go swimming,' and I said, 'Okay, let's,' and . . ." There was a pause while Peyton found an orange crayon. "And Barbie said, 'Let's go!' and we went swimming." She began drawing a row of rapid sideways zigzags.

"Is that her swimming suit?" I asked.

"No-o-o," she said. "That's Barbie."

Barbie? I thought, wondering what the symbolism of the zigzags was. Of course. Barbie's high heels.

"So the next day," Peyton said, selecting yellow orange and drawing spiky suns, "Barbie said, 'Let's go shopping,' and I said, 'Okay, let's,' and she said, 'Let's ride our mopeds,' and I said—"

Billy Ray came out of his tunnel, and I got the phone switched on almost before it rang. "So you're on your way to Denver?" I said.

"Nope. Other direction. Durango. Conference on teleconferences. I got to thinking about you and thought I'd call. Do you ever get to hankering for something besides what you're doing?"

"Yes," I said fervently, reading the names of the crayons Peyton had discarded. Periwinkle. Screamin' green. Cerulean blue.

"—so Barbie said, 'Hi, Ken,' and Ken said, 'Hi, Barbie, want to go on a date?' " Peyton said, busily drawing lines.

"Me too," Billy Ray said. "I've been thinking, is this really what I want?"

"Didn't the sheep work out?"

"The Targhees? No, they're doing fine. It's this whole ranching thing. It's so isolated."

Except for the fax and the net and the cell phone, I thought.

". . . so Barbie said, 'I don't want to be in time-out,' " Peyton said, wielding a black crayon. " 'Okay,' Barbie's mom said, 'you don't have to.' "

"Do you ever get to feeling . . . ," Billy Ray said, ". . . kinda . . . I don't know what to call it . . ."

I do, I thought. Itch. And does that mean this unsettled, dissatisfied feeling is some sort of fad, too, like tattoos and violets? And if so, how did it get started?

I sat up straighter on the bed. "When exactly did you start having this feeling?" I asked him, but there was already an ominous hum from the cell phone.

"Another tunnel," Billy Ray said. "We'll talk about it some more when I get back. I've got something I want to—" and the phone went dead.

Lindsay's mother had talked about feeling itch, and so had Flip, that day in the coffeehouse, and I had felt so vaguely longing I'd gone out with Billy Ray. Had I spread the feeling on to him, like some kind of virus, and was that how fads spread, by infection?

"Your turn," Peyton said, holding out a neon-red crayon. Radical red.

"Okay," I said, taking the crayon. "So Barbie decided to go to . . ." I drew a line of radical red high heels across the blue scallops. ". . . the barbershop. 'I want my hair bobbed,' she said to the barber." I started a line of aquamarine scissors. "And the barber said, 'Why?' And Barbie said, 'Because everybody else is doing it.' So the barber chopped off Barbie's hair and—"

"*No-o,*" Peyton said, grabbing the aquamarine away from me and handing me laser lemon. "*This* is Cut 'n' Curl Barbie."

"Oh," I said. "Okay. So the barber said, 'But somebody had to do it first, and *they* couldn't do it because everybody else was doing it, so why did *they*'—"

There was a sound at the door, and Peyton snatched the laser lemon out of my hand, flipped the tablet shut, stowed them both under the bed with amazing speed, and was sitting on the edge of it with her hands folded in her lap when her mother opened the door.

"Peyton, we're watching a video now. Do—" she said, and stopped when she saw me. "You didn't talk to Peyton while she was in her time-out, did you?"

"Not a word," I said.

She turned back to Peyton. "Do you think you can exhibit positive peer behavior now?"

Peyton nodded wisely and tore out of the room, her mother following. I put the phone back on the nightstand and started after her, and then stopped and recovered the tablet from its hiding place and looked at it again.

It was a map, in spite of what Peyton had said. A combination map and diagram and picture, with an amazing amount of information packed onto one page: location, time elapsed, outfits worn. An amazing amount of data.

And it intersected in interesting ways, the lines crossing and recrossing to form elaborate intersections, radical red changing to lavender and orange in overlay. Barbie only rode her moped in the lower half of the picture, and there was a solid knot of stars in one corner. A statistical anomaly?

I wondered if a diagram-map-story like this would work for my twenties data. I'd tried maps and statistical charts and computational models, but never all three together, color-coded for date and vector and incidence. If I put it all together, what kinds of patterns would emerge?

There was a shriek from the living room. "It's *my* birthday!" Brittany wailed.

I tucked the tablet back under the bed.

"My, Peyton," Lindsay's mother said. "What a creative way to show your need for attention."

pyrography (1900–05)——— Craft fad in which designs were burned into wood or leather with a hot iron. Flowers, birds, horses, and knights in armor were branded onto pin cases, pen trays, glove boxes, pipe racks, playing card cases, and other similarly useless items. Died out because its ability threshold was too high. Everyone's horses looked like cows.

Thursday the weather got worse. It was spitting snow when I got to work, and by lunch it was a full-blown blizzard. Flip had managed to break both copy machines, so I gathered up my flagpole-sitting clippings to be copied at Kinko's, but as I walked out to my car I decided they could wait, and I scuttled back to the building, my head down against the snow. And practically ran into Shirl.

She was huddled next to a minivan, smoking a cigarette. She had a brown mitten on the hand that wasn't holding the cigarette, her coat collar was turned up, a muffler was wrapped around her chin, and she was shivering.

"Shirl!" I shouted against the wind. "What are you doing out here?"

She clumsily fished a piece of paper out of her coat pocket with her mittened hand and handed it to me. It was a memo declaring the entire building smoke-free.

"Flip," I said, shaking snow off the already wet memo. "She's behind this." I crumpled the memo up and threw it on the ground. "Don't you have a car?" I said.

She shook her head, shivering. "I get a ride to work."

"You can sit in my car," I said, and thought of a better place. "Come on." I took hold of her arm. "I know someplace you can smoke."

"The whole building's been declared off-limits to smoking," she said, resisting.

"This place isn't in the building," I said.

She stubbed out her cigarette. "This is a kind thing to do for an old lady," she said, and we both scuttled back to the building through the driving snow.

We stopped inside the door to shake the snow off and take off our hats. Her leathery face was bright red with cold.

"You don't have to do this," she said, unwrapping her muffler.

"When you've spent as much time studying fads as I have, you develop a hearty dislike for them," I said. "Especially aversion fads. They seem to bring out the worst in people. And it's the principle of the thing. Next it might be chocolate cheesecake. Or reading. Come on."

I led her down the hall. "This place won't be warm, but it'll be out of the wind, and you won't get snowed on, at least. And this antismoking fad should be dying out by spring. It's reaching the extreme stage that inevitably produces a backlash."

"Prohibition lasted thirteen years."

"The law did. The fad didn't. McCarthyism only lasted four." I started down the stairs to Bio.

"Where exactly is this place?" Shirl asked.

"It's Dr. O'Reilly's lab," I said. "It's got a porch out back with an overhang."

"And you're sure he won't mind?"

"I'm sure," I said. "He never pays any attention to what other people think."

"He sounds like an extraordinary young man," Shirl said, and I thought, He really is.

He didn't fit any of the usual patterns. He certainly wasn't a rebel, refusing to go along with fads to assert his individuality. Rebellion can be a fad, too, as witness Hell's Angels and peace symbols. And yet he wasn't oblivious either. He was funny and intelligent and observant.

I tried to explain that to Shirl as we went downstairs to Bio. "It isn't that he doesn't care what other people think. It's just that he doesn't see what it has to do with him."

"My physics teacher used to say Diogenes shouldn't have wasted his time looking for an honest man," Shirl said, "he should have been looking for somebody who thought for himself."

I started down Bio's hall, and it suddenly occurred to me that Alicia might be in the lab. "Wait here a sec," I said to Shirl, and peeked in the door. "Bennett?"

He was hunched over his desk, practically hidden by papers.

"Can Shirl smoke out on the porch?" I said.

"Sure," he said without looking up.

I went out and got Shirl.

"You can smoke in here if you want," Bennett said when we came in.

"No, she can't. HiTek's made the whole building nonsmoking," I said. "I told her she could smoke out on the porch."

"Sure," he said, standing up. "Feel free to come down here anytime. I'm always here."

"Oh?" Shirl said. "You work on your project even during lunch?"

He told her he didn't have a project to work on and he

had to wait for his funding to be approved before he could get his macaques, but I wasn't paying attention. I was looking at what he was wearing.

Flip had been right about Bennett. He was wearing a white shirt and a Cerenkhov blue tie.

"I've been working on this chaos thing," he said, straightening the tie.

"Did Alicia decide chaos theory was the optimum project to win the Niebnitz Grant?" I said, and couldn't keep the sharpness out of my voice.

"No," he said, frowning at me. "When she was talking about variables the other day, it gave me an idea about why my prediction rate didn't improve. So I refigured the data."

"And did it help?" I said.

"No," he said, looking abstracted, the way he had when Alicia'd been talking. "The more work I do on it, the more I think maybe Verhoest was right, and there is an outside force acting on the system." He said to Shirl, "You're probably not interested in this. Here, let me show you where the porch is." He led her through the habitat to the back door. "When my macaques come, you'll have to go around the side." He opened the door, and snow and wind whirled in. "Are you sure you don't want to smoke inside? You could stand in the door. Leave the door open at least so there's some heat."

"I was born in Montana," she said, wrapping her muffler around her neck as she went out. "This is a mild summer breeze," but I noticed she left the door open.

Bennett came back in, rubbing his arms. "*Brr*, it's freezing out there. What's the matter with people? Sending an old lady out in the snow in the name of moral righteousness. I suppose Flip was behind it."

"Flip is behind everything." I looked at the littered desk. "I guess I'd better let you get back to work. Thanks for letting Shirl smoke down here."

"No, wait," he said. "I had a couple of things I wanted to ask you about the funding form." He scrabbled through the stuff on his desk and came up with the form. He flipped through pages, looking. "Page fifty-one, section eight. What does *Documentation Scatter Method* mean?"

"You're supposed to put down *ALR-Augmented*," I said.

"What does that mean?"

"I have no idea. It's what Gina told me to put."

He penciled it in, shaking his head. "These funding forms are going to be the death of me. I could have *done* the project in the time it's taken me to fill out this form. HiTek wants us to win the Niebnitz Grant, to make scientific breakthroughs. But name me one scientist who ever made a significant breakthrough while filling out a funding form. Or attending a meeting."

"Mendeleev," Shirl said.

We both turned around. Shirl was standing inside the door, shaking snow off her hat. "Mendeleev was on his way to a cheesemaking conference when he solved the problem of the periodic chart," she said.

"That's right, he was," Bennett said. "He stepped on the train and the solution came to him, just like that."

"Like Poincaré," I said. "Only he stepped on a bus."

"And discovered Fuchsian functions," Bennett said.

"Kekulé was on a bus, too, wasn't he, when he discovered the benzene ring," Shirl said thoughtfully. "In Ghent."

"He was," I said, surprised. "How do you know so much about science, Shirl?"

"I have to make copies of so many scientific reports, I figured I might as well read them," she said. "Didn't Einstein look at the town clock from a bus while he was working on relativity?"

"A bus," I said. "Maybe that's what you and I need, Bennett. We take a bus someplace and suddenly everything's clear—you know what's wrong with your chaos data and I know what caused hair-bobbing."

"That sounds like a great idea," Bennett said. "Let's—"

"Oh, good, you're here, Bennett," Alicia said. "I need to talk to you about the grant profile. Shirl, make five copies of this." She dumped a stack of papers into Shirl's arms. "Collated and stapled. And this time don't put them on my desk. Put them in my mailbox." She turned back to Bennett. "I need you to help me come up with additional relevant factors."

"Transportation," I said, and started for the door. "And cheese."

ironing hair (1965—68)———Hair fad inspired by Joan Baez, Mary Travers, and other folksingers. Part of the hippie fad, the lank look of long straight hair was harder to obtain than the male's general shagginess. Beauty parlors gave "antiperms," but the preferred method among teenagers was laying their heads on the ironing board and pressing their locks with a clothes iron. The ironing was done a few inches at a time by a friend (who hopefully knew what she was doing), and college girls lined up in dorms to take their turns.

During the next few days, nothing much happened. The simplified funding allocation forms were due on the twenty-third, and, after donating yet another weekend to filling them out, I gave mine to Flip to deliver and then thought better of it and took it up to Paperwork myself.

The weather turned nice again, Elaine tried to talk me into going white-water rafting with her to relieve stress, Sarah told me her boyfriend, Ted, was experiencing attachment aversion, Gina asked me if I knew where to find Romantic Bride Barbie for Bethany (who had decided she wanted one just like Brittany's and whose birthday was in November), and I got three overdue notices for Browning, *The Complete Works*.

In between, I finished entering all my King Tut and black

bottom data and started drawing a Barbie picture. I didn't have a box of sixty-four crayons, but there was a paintbox on the computer. I called it up, along with my statistical and differential equations programs, and started coding the correlations and plotting the relationships to each other. I graphed skirt lengths in cerulean blue, cigarette sales in gray, plotted lavender regressions for Isadora Duncan and yellow ones for temps above eighty-five. White for Irene Castle, radical red for references to rouge, brown for "Bernice Bobs Her Hair."

Flip came in periodically to hand me petitions and ask me questions like, "If you had a fairy godmother, what would she look like?"

"An old lady," I said, thinking of *Toads and Diamonds*, "or a bird, or something ugly, like a toad. Fairy godmothers disguise themselves so they can tell if you're deserving of help by whether you're nice to them. What do you need one for?"

She rolled her eyes. "You're not supposed to ask interdepartmental communications liaisons personal questions. If they're in disguise, how do you know to be nice to them?"

"You're supposed to be nice in general—" I said and realized it was hopeless. "What's the petition for?"

"It's to make HiTek give us dental insurance, of course," she said.

Of course.

"You don't think it's my assistant, do you?" Flip said. "She's an old lady."

I handed her back the petition. "I doubt very much that Shirl is your fairy godmother in disguise."

"*Good*," she said. "There's no way I'm going to be nice to somebody who *smokes*."

I didn't see Bennett, who was busy preparing for the arrival of his macaques, or Shirl, who was doing all Flip's work, but I did see Alicia. She came up to the lab, wearing po-mo pink, and demanded to borrow my computer.

"Flip's using mine," she said irately, "and when I told her to get off, she *refused*. Have you ever met anyone who was that rude?"

That was a tough one. "How's the search for the Philosopher's Stone going?" I said.

"I've definitely eliminated circumstantial predisposition as a criterion," she said, shifting my data to the lab table. "Only two Niebnitz Grant recipients have ever made a significant scientific breakthrough subsequent to their winning of the award. And I've narrowed down the project approach to a cross-discipline-designed experiment, but I still haven't determined the personal profile. I'm still evaluating the variables." She popped my disk out and shoved her own in.

"Have you taken disease into account?" I said.

She looked irritated. "Disease?"

"Diseases have played a big part in scientific breakthroughs. Einstein's measles, Mendeleev's lung trouble, Darwin's hypochondria. The bubonic plague. They closed down Cambridge because of it, and Newton had to go back home to the apple orchard."

"I hardly see—"

"And what about their shooting skills?"

"If you're trying to be funny—"

"Fleming's rifle-shooting skills were why St. Mary's wanted him to stay on after he graduated as a surgeon. They needed him for the hospital rifle team, only there wasn't an opening in surgery, so they offered him a job in microbiology."

"And what exactly does Fleming have to do with the Niebnitz Grant?"

"He was circumstantially predisposed to significant scientific breakthroughs. What about their exercise habits? James Watt solved the steam engine problem while he was taking a walk, and William Rowan Hamilton—"

Alicia snatched up her papers and ejected her disk. "I'll use someone else's computer," she said. "It may interest you to know that statistically, fad research has absolutely no chance at all."

Yes, well, I knew that. Particularly the way it was going right now. Not only did my diagram not look nearly as good as Peyton's, but no butterfly outlines had appeared. Except the Marydale, Ohio, one, which was not only still there, but had been reinforced by the rolled-down stockings and crossword puzzle data.

But there was nothing for it but to keep slogging through the crocodile- and tsetse fly–infested tributaries. I calculated prediction intervals on Couéism and the crossword puzzle, and then started feeding in the related hairstyle data.

I couldn't find the clippings on the marcel wave. I'd given them to Flip a week and a half ago, along with the angel data and the personal ads. And hadn't seen any of it since.

I sorted through the stacks next to the computer on the off chance she'd brought it back and just dumped it somewhere, and then tracked Flip down in Supply, making long strands of Desiderata's hair into hair wraps.

"The other day I gave you a bunch of stuff to copy," I said to Flip. "There were some articles about angels and a bunch of clippings about hair-bobbing. What did you do with them?"

Flip rolled her eyes. "How would I know?"

"Because I gave them to you to copy. Because I *need* them, and they're not in my lab. There were some clippings about marcel waves," I persisted. "Remember? The wavy hairdo you liked?" I made a series of crimping motions next to my hair, hoping she'd remember, but she was wrapping Desiderata's wrappers with duct tape. "There was a page of personal ads, too."

That clearly rang a bell. She and Desiderata exchanged looks, and she said, "So now you're accusing me of stealing?"

"Stealing?" I said blankly. Angel articles and marcel wave clippings?

"They're public, you know. Anybody can write in."

I had no idea what she was talking about. Public?

"Just because you circled him doesn't mean he's yours." She yanked on Desiderata's hair. Desiderata yelped. "Besides, you already have that rodeo guy."

The personals, I thought, the light dawning. We're talking about the personal ads. Which explained her asking me about *elegant* and *sophisticated*. "You answered one of the personal ads?" I said.

"Like you didn't know. Like you and Darrell didn't have a big laugh over it," she said, and flung down the duct tape and ran out of the room.

I looked at Desiderata, who was trailing a long ragged end of duct tape from the hair wrap. "What was that all about?" I said.

"He lives on Valmont," she said.

"And?" I said, wishing I understood at least something that was said to me.

"Flip lives south of Baseline."

I was still looking blank.

Desiderata sighed. "Don't you *get* it? She's geographically incompatible."

She also has an *i* on her forehead, I thought, which somebody looking for elegant and sophisticated must have found daunting. "His name's Darrell?" I asked.

Desiderata nodded, trying to wind the end of the duct tape around her hair. "He's a dentist."

The crown, I thought. Of course.

"I think he's totally swarb, but Flip really likes him."

It was hard to imagine Flip liking anyone, and we were getting off the main issue. She had taken the personal ads, and done what with the rest of the articles? "You don't know where she might have put my marcel wave clippings, do you?"

"Gosh, no," Desiderata said. "Did you look in your lab?"

I gave up and went down to the copy room to try to find them myself. Flip apparently never copied anything. There were huge piles on both sides of the copier, on top of the copier lid, and on every flat surface in the room, including two waist-high piles on the floor, stacked in layers like sedimentary rock formations.

I sat down cross-legged on the floor and started through them: memos, reports, a hundred copies of a sensitivity exercise that started with "List five things you like about HiTek," a letter marked URGENT and dated July 6, 1988.

I found some notes I'd taken on Pet Rocks and the receipt from somebody's paycheck, but no marcel waves. I scooted over and started on the next stack.

"Sandy," a man's voice said from the door.

I looked up. Bennett was standing there. Something was clearly wrong. His sandy hair was awry and his face was gray under his freckles.

"What is it?" I said, scrambling to my feet.

He gestured, a little wildly, at the sheaf of papers in my hand. "You didn't find my funding allocation application in there, did you?"

"Your funding allocation form?" I said bewilderedly. "It had to be turned in Monday."

"I *know*," he said, raking his hand through his hair. "I did turn it in. I gave it to Flip."

4. rapids

I suppose God could have made
a sillier animal than a sheep,
but it is very certain
that He never did. . . .

dorothy sayers

Jitterbug (1938—45)——Dance fad of World War II, involving fancy footwork and athletic moves. Danced to bigband swing tunes, jitterbuggers flung their partners over their backs, under their legs, and into the air. GIs spread the jitterbug overseas wherever they were stationed. Replaced by the cha-cha.

Catastrophes can sometimes lead to scientific breakthroughs. A contaminated culture and a near drowning led to the discovery of penicillin, ruined photographic plates to the discovery of X rays. Take Mendeleev. His whole life was a series of catastrophes: He lived in Siberia, his father went blind, and the glass factory his mother started to make ends meet after his father died burned to the ground. But it was that fire that made his mother move to St. Petersburg, where Mendeleev was able to study with Bunsen and, eventually, come up with the periodic table of the elements.

Or take James Christy. He had a more minor catastrophe to deal with: a broken Star Scan machine. He'd just taken a picture of Pluto and was getting ready to throw it away because of a clearly wrong bulge at the edge of the planet when the Star Scan (obviously made by the same company as HiTek's copy machines) crashed.

Instead of throwing the photographic plate away, Christy had to call the repairman, who asked Christy to wait in case he needed help. Christy stood around for a while and then took another, harder look at the bulge and decided to check some of the earlier photographs. The very first one he found was marked "Pluto image. Elongated. Plate no good. Reject." He compared it to the one in his hand. The plates looked the same, and Christy realized he was looking not at ruined pictures, but at a moon of Pluto.

On the whole, though, catastrophes are just catastrophes. Like this one.

Management cares about only one thing. Paperwork. They will forgive almost anything else—cost overruns, gross incompetence, criminal indictments—as long as the paperwork's filled out properly. And in on time.

"You gave your funding allocation form to *Flip*?" I said, and was instantly sorry.

He went even paler. "I know. Stupid, huh?"

"Your monkeys," I said.

"My ex-monkeys. I will not be teaching them the Hula Hoop." He went over to the stack I'd just been through and started through it.

"I've already been through those," I said. "It's not in there. Did you tell Management Flip lost it?"

"Yes," he said, picking up the papers on top of the copier. "Management said Flip says she turned in all the applications people gave her."

"And they *believed* her?" I said. Well, of course they believed her. They'd believed her when she said she needed an assistant. "Is anybody else's form missing?"

"No," he said grimly. "Of the three people stupid enough to let Flip turn their forms in, I'm the only one whose form she lost."

"Maybe . . . ," I said.

"I already asked them. I can't redo it and turn it in late."
He set down the stack, picked it up, and started through it
again.

"Look," I said, taking it from him. "Let's take this in an
orderly fashion. You go through these piles." I set it next to
the stack I'd gone through. "Stacks we've looked through on
this side of the room." I handed him one of the worktable
stacks. "Stuff we haven't on this side. Okay?"

"Okay," he said, and I thought a little of his color came
back. He picked up the top of the stack.

I started through the recycling bin, into which somebody
(very probably Flip) had dropped a half-full can of Coke. I
grabbed a sticky armful of papers, sat down on the floor, and
began pulling them apart. It wasn't in the first armload. I bent
over the bin and grabbed a second, hoping the Coke hadn't
trickled all the way to the bottom. It had.

"I knew better than to give it to Flip," Bennett said, starting on another stack, "but I was working on my chaos theory
data, and she told me she was supposed to take them up to
Management."

"We'll find it," I said, prying a Coke-gummed page free
from the wad. Halfway through the papers I gave a yelp.

"Did you find it?" he said hopefully.

"No. Sorry." I showed him the sticky pages. "It's the
marcel wave notes I was looking for. I gave them to Flip to
copy."

The color went completely out of his face, freckles and all.
"She threw the application away," he said.

"No, she didn't," I said, trying not to think about all those
crumpled hair-bobbing clippings in my wastebasket the day I
met Bennett. "It's here somewhere."

It wasn't. We finished the stacks and went through them
even though it was obvious the form wasn't there.

"Could she have left it in your lab?" I said when I reached

the bottom of the last stack. "Maybe she never made it out of there with it."

He shook his head. "I've already been through the whole place. Twice," he said, digging through the wastebasket. "What about your lab? She delivered that package to you. Maybe—"

I hated having to disappoint him. "I just ransacked it. Looking for these." I held up my marcel wave clippings. "It could be in somebody else's lab, though." I got up stiffly. "What about Flip? Did you ask her what she did with it? What am I thinking? This is Flip we're talking about."

He nodded. "She said, 'What funding form?'"

"All right," I said. "We need a plan of attack. You take the cafeteria, and I'll take the staff lounge."

"The cafeteria?"

"Yes, you know Flip," I said. "She probably misdelivered it. Like that package the day I met you," and I felt there was a clue there, something significant not to where his funding form might be, but to something else. The thing that had triggered hair-bobbing? No, that wasn't it. I stood there, trying to hold the feeling.

"What is it?" Bennett said. "Do you think you know where it is?"

It was gone. "No. Sorry. I was just thinking about something else. I'll meet you at the recycling bin over in Chem. Don't worry. We'll find it," I said cheerfully, but I didn't have much hope that we actually would. Knowing Flip, she could have left it anywhere. HiTek was huge. It could be in anybody's lab. Or down in Supply with Desiderata, the patron saint of lost objects. Or out in the parking lot. "Meet you at the recycling bin."

I started up to the staff lounge and then had a better idea. I went to find Shirl. She was in Alicia's lab, typing Niebnitz Grant data into the computer.

"Flip lost Dr. O'Reilly's funding form," I said without preamble.

I had somehow hoped she would say, "I know right where it is," but she didn't. She said, "Oh, dear," and looked genuinely upset. "If he leaves, that—" She stopped. "What can I do to help?"

"Look in here," I said. "Bennett's in here a lot, and anyplace you can think of where she might have put it."

"But the deadline's past, isn't it?"

"Yes," I said, angry that she was pointing out the thought I'd been trying to ignore, that Management, sticklers for deadlines that they were, would refuse to accept it even if we did find it, sticky with Coke and obviously mislaid. "I'll be up in the staff lounge," I said, and went up to look through the mailboxes.

It wasn't there, or in the stack of old memos on the staff table, or in the microwave. Or in Alicia's lab. "I looked all through it," Shirl said, sticking her head in. "What day did Dr. O'Reilly give it to Flip?"

"I don't know," I said. "It was due on Monday."

She shook her head grimly. "That's what I was afraid of. The trash comes on Tuesdays and Thursdays."

I was sorry I'd brought her into this. I went down to the recycling bin. Bennett was almost all the way inside it, his legs dangling in midair. He came up with a fistful of papers and an apple core.

I took half the papers, and we went through them. No funding form.

"All right," I said, trying to sound upbeat. "If it's not in here, it's in one of the labs. What shall we start with? Chem or Physics?"

"It's no use," Bennett said wearily. He sank back against the bin. "It's not here, and I'm not here for much longer."

"Isn't there some way to do the project without funding?"

I said. "You've got the habitat and the computer and cameras and everything. Couldn't you substitute lab rats or something?"

He shook his head. "They're too independent. I need an animal with a strong herd instinct."

What about "The Pied Piper"? I thought.

"And even lab rats cost money," he said.

"What about the pound?" I said. "They've probably got cats. No, not cats. Dogs. Dogs have pack behavior, and the pound has lots of dogs."

He was looking almost as disgusted as Flip. "I thought you were an expert on fads. Haven't you ever heard of animal rights?"

"But you're not going to do anything to them. You're just going to observe them," I said, but he was right. I'd forgotten about the animal rights movement. They'd never let us use animals from the pound. "What about the other Bio projects? Maybe you could borrow some of their lab animals."

"Dr. Kelly's working with nematodes, and Dr. Riez is working with flatworms."

And Dr. Turnbull's working on ways to win the Niebnitz Grant, I thought.

"Besides," he said, "even if I had animals, I couldn't feed them. I didn't get my funding form in on time, remember? It's okay," he said at the look on my face. "This'll give me a chance to go back to chaos theory."

For which there isn't any funding, I thought, even if you do turn in the forms.

"Well," he said, standing up. "I'd better go start typing my résumé."

He looked at me seriously. "Thanks again for helping me. I mean it." He started down the hall.

"Don't give up yet," I said. "I'll think of something." This from someone who couldn't figure out what had caused the angels fad, let alone hair-bobbing.

He shook his head. "We're up against Flip here. It's bigger than both of us."

chain letters (spring 1935)—— Moneymaking fad which involved sending a dime to the name at the top of a list, adding your name to the bottom, and sending five copies of the letter to friends, who, hopefully, were as gullible as you were. Caused by greed and a lack of understanding of statistics, the fad sprang up in Denver, deluging the post office with nearly a hundred thousand letters a day. It lasted three weeks in Denver, then moved on to Springfield, where dollar and five-dollar chains circulated for a frenzied two weeks before the inevitable collapse. Mutated into Circle of Gold (1978), which passed the letters in person, and various pyramid schemes.

I watched him go and then went back up to my lab. Flip was there on my computer. "How do you spell *adorable*?" she asked.

It took all my willpower not to shake her till her *i* rattled. "*What* did you do with Dr. O'Reilly's funding form?"

She tossed her assortment of hair appendages. "I *told* Desiderata you'd take it out on me for stealing your boyfriend. Which is not fair. You already have that cow guy."

"Sheep," I corrected automatically, and then gaped at her. Sheep.

"Telling an interdepartmental communications liaison

who they can write letters to is har*ass*ment," she said, but I didn't hear her. I was punching in Billy Ray's number.

"Boy, am I glad to hear your voice," Billy Ray said. "I've been thinking about you a lot lately."

"Could I borrow some sheep?" I said, not listening to him either.

"Sure," he said. "What for?"

"A learning experiment."

"How many do you need?"

"How many does it take before they act like a flock?"

"Three. When do you want them?"

He really was a very nice guy. "A couple of weeks," I said. "I'm not sure. I need to check some things out first. Like how big a flock we can have in the paddock." And I need to get Bennett to agree. And Management.

"Drawing a circle doesn't make somebody somebody's *prop*erty," Flip said.

I ran back down to Bio. Bennett wasn't typing up his résumé. He was sitting on a rock in the middle of the habitat, looking depressed.

"Ben," I said, "I have a proposition for you."

He almost smiled. "Thanks, but—"

"Listen," I said, "and don't say no till you hear the whole thing. I want us to combine our projects. No, wait, hear me out. I asked for funding for a higher-memory-capacity computer, but I could use yours. Flip's always on mine anyway. And then we could use my funding to buy the food and supplies."

"That still doesn't solve the problem of the macaques. Unless you asked for an awfully expensive computer."

"I have a friend who has a sheep ranch in Wyoming," I said.

"Yeah, I know," he said.

"He's willing to loan us as many sheep as we need, no

cost, we just have to feed them." He looked like he was getting set to refuse, and I hurried on. "I know sheep don't have the social organization of macaques, but they do have a very strong following instinct. What one of them does, they all want to do. And they withstand cold, so they can be outside."

He was looking at me seriously through his thick glasses.

"I know it's not the project you wanted to do, but it would be something. It would keep you from leaving HiTek, and it'll probably only be a few months till Management comes up with a new acronym and a new funding procedure, and you can put in for your macaques again."

"I don't know anything about sheep."

"We can do all the background research while we're waiting for the paperwork to go through."

"And what do you get out of it, Sandy?" Ben said. "Sheep have their hair bobbed for them."

I couldn't very well tell him I thought his immunity to fads was part of the key to where fads came from. "A computer I can run these new diagrams I thought of on," I said. "And a different perspective. I'm not getting anywhere with my hair-bobbing project. Richard Feynman said if you're stuck on a scientific problem, you should work on something else for a while. It gives you a different angle on the problem. He took up the bongo drums. And a lot of scientists make their most significant scientific breakthroughs when they're working outside their own field. Look at Alfred Wegener, who discovered continental drift. He was a meteorologist, not a geologist. And Joseph Black, who discovered carbon dioxide, wasn't a chemist. He was a doctor. Einstein was a patent official. Working outside their fields makes scientists see connections they never would have seen before."

"Umm," Ben said. "And there definitely is a connection between sheep and people who follow fads."

"Right. Who knows? Maybe the sheep will start a fad."

"Flagpole-sitting?"

"The crossword puzzle. A three-letter word for a lab animal. *Ewe*." I smiled at him. "And even if they don't, it'll be a positive relief to work with them. Except for Mary and her little lamb, sheep have never been a fad. So what do you think?"

He smiled sadly. "I think Management will never go for it."

"But if they did?"

"If they did, I can't think of anything I'd rather do than work with you. But they won't. And even if they did, it'll take months to fill out all the paperwork, let alone wait for it to go through."

"Then it would give us *both* a different perspective. Remember Mendeleev and the cheesemaking conference."

"How do you suggest we go about telling Management your proposition?" he said.

"You leave that part to me. You go to work on adapting the project to work with sheep. I'll go talk to an expert," I said, and went up to see Gina.

She was addressing bright pink Barbie invitations. "I still can't find a Romantic Bride Barbie anywhere. I've called five different toystores."

I told her what had happened.

She shook her head sadly. "Too bad. I always liked him— even if he didn't have any fashion sense."

"I need your help," I said. I told her about combining the projects.

"So he gets your funding and Billy Ray's sheep," she said. "What do you get out of it?"

"A minor victory over Flip and the forces of chaos," I said. "It isn't fair for him to lose his funding just because Flip is incompetent."

She gave me a long, considering look, and then shook her

head. "Management'll never go for it. First, it's live-animal research, which is controversial. Management hates controversy. Second, it's something innovative, which means Management will hate it on principle."

"I thought one of the keystones of GRIM was innovation."

"Are you kidding? If it's new, Management doesn't have a form for it, and Management loves forms almost as much as they hate controversy. Sorry," she said. "I know you like him." She went back to addressing envelopes.

"If you'll help me, I'll find Romantic Barbie for you," I said.

She looked up from the invitations. "It has to be Romantic Bride Barbie. Not Country Bride Barbie or Wedding Fantasy Barbie."

I nodded. "Is it a deal?"

"I can't guarantee Management will go for it even if I help you," she said, shoving the invitations to the side and handing me a notepad and pencil. "All right, tell me what you were going to tell Management."

"Well, I thought I'd start by explaining what happened to the funding form—"

"Wrong," she said. "They'll know what you're up to in a minute. You tell them you've been working on this joint project thing since the meeting before last, when they said how important staff input and interaction were. Use words like *optimize* and *patterning systems*."

"Okay," I said, taking notes.

"Tell them any number of scientific breakthroughs have been made by scientists working together. Crick and Watson, Penzias and Wilson, Gilbert and Sullivan—"

I looked up from my notes. "Gilbert and Sullivan weren't scientists."

"Management won't know that. And they might recognize the name. You'll need a two-page prospectus of the project goals. Put anything you think they'll think is a problem on the second page. They never read the second page."

"You mean an outline of the project?" I said, scribbling. "Explaining the experimental method we're going to use and describing the connection between trends analysis and information diffusion research?"

"No," she said, and turned around to her computer. "Never mind, I'll write it for you." She began typing rapidly. "You tell them integrated cross-discipline teaming projects are the latest thing at MIT. Tell them single-person projects are passé." She hit PRINT, and a sheet started scrolling through the printer.

"And pay attention to Management's body language. If he taps his forefinger on the desk, you're in trouble."

She handed me the prospectus. It looked suspiciously like her five all-purpose objectives, which meant it would probably work.

"And don't wear that." She pointed at my skirt and lab coat. "You're supposed to be dressing down."

"Thanks," I said. "Do you think this'll do it?"

"When it's live-animal research?" she said. "Are you kidding? Romantic Bride Barbie is the one with the pink net roses," she said. "Oh, and Bethany wants a brunette one."

mah-jongg (1922—24)——American game fad inspired by the ancient Chinese tiles game. As played by Americans, it was a sort of cross between rummy and dominoes involving building walls and then breaking them down, and "catching the moon from the bottom of the sea." There were enthusiastic calls of "Pung!" and "Chow!" and much clattering of ivory tiles. Players dressed up in Oriental robes (sometimes, if the players were unclear on the concept of China, these were Japanese kimonos) and served tea. Although superseded by the crossword puzzle craze and contract bridge, mah-jongg continued to be popular among Jewish matrons until the 1960s.

I had failed to include all the variables. It was true that Management values paperwork more than anything. Except for the Niebnitz Grant.

I had hardly started into my spiel in Management's white-carpeted office when Management's eyes lit up, and he said, "This would be a cross-discipline project?"

"Yes," I said. "Trends analysis combined with learning vectors in higher mammals. And there are certain aspects of chaos theory—"

"Chaos theory?" he said, tapping his forefinger on his expensive teak desk.

"Only in the sense that these are nonlinear systems which require a designed experiment," I said hastily. "The emphasis is primarily on information diffusion in higher mammals, of which human trends are a subset."

"Designed experiment?" he said eagerly.

"Yes. The practical value to HiTek would be better understanding of how information spreads through human societies and—"

"What was your original field?" he cut in.

"Statistics," I said. "The advantages of using sheep over macaques are—" and never got to finish because Management was already standing up and shaking my hand.

"This is exactly the kind of project that GRIM is all about. Interfacing scientific disciplines, implementing initiative and cooperation to create new workplace paradigms."

He actually talks in acronyms, I thought wonderingly, and almost missed what he said next.

"—exactly the kind of project the Niebnitz Grant Committee is looking for. I want this project implemented immediately. How soon can you have it up and running?"

"I—it—" I stammered. "There's some background research we'll need to do on sheep behavior. And there are the live-animal regulations that have to be—"

He waved an airy hand. "It'll be our problem to deal with that. I want you and Dr. O'Reilly to concentrate on that divergent thinking and scientific sensibility. I expect great things." He shook my hand enthusiastically. "HiTek is going to do everything we can to cut right through the red tape and get this project on line immediately."

And did.

Permissions were typed up, paperwork waived, and live-animal approvals filed for almost before I could get down to Bio and tell Bennett they'd approved the project.

"What does 'on line immediately' mean?" he said worriedly. "We haven't done any background research on sheep behavior, how they interact, what skills they're capable of learning, what they eat—"

"We'll have plenty of time," I said. "This is Management, remember?"

Wrong again. Friday Management called me on the white carpet again and told me the permissions had all been gotten, the live-animal approvals approved. "Can you have the sheep here by Monday?"

"I'll need to see if the owner can arrange it," I said, hoping Billy Ray couldn't.

He could, and did, though he didn't bring them down himself. He was attending a virtual ranching meeting in Lander. He sent instead Miguel, who had a nose ring, Aussie hat, headphones, and no intention of unloading the sheep.

"Where do you want them?" he said in a tone that made me peer under the brim of the Aussie hat to see if he had an *i* on his forehead.

We showed him the paddock gate, and he sighed heavily, backed the truck more or less up to it, and then stood against the truck's cab looking put-upon.

"Aren't you going to unload them?" Ben said finally.

"Billy Ray told me to deliver them," Miguel said. "He didn't say anything about unloading them."

"You should meet our mail clerk," I said. "You're obviously made for each other."

He tipped the Aussie hat forward warily. "Where does she live?"

Bennett had gone around to the back of the truck and was lifting the bar that held the door shut. "You don't suppose they'll all come rushing out at once and trample us, do you?" he said.

No. The thirty or so sheep stood on the edge of the truck bed, bleating and looking terrified.

"Come on," Ben said coaxingly. "Do you think it's too far for them to jump?"

"They jumped off a cliff in *Far from the Madding Crowd*," I said. "How can it be too far?"

Nevertheless, Ben went to get a piece of plywood for a makeshift ramp, and I went to see if Dr. Riez, who had done an equine experiment before he turned to flatworms, had a halter we could borrow.

It took him forever to find a halter, and I figured by the time I got back to the lab it would no longer be needed, but the sheep were still huddled in the back of the truck.

Ben was looking frustrated, and Miguel, up by the front of the truck, was swaying to some unheard rhythm.

"They won't come," Ben said. "I've tried calling and coaxing and whistling."

I handed him the halter.

"Maybe if we can get one down the ramp," he said, "they'll all follow." He took the halter and went up the ramp. "Get out of the way in case they all make a mad dash."

He reached to slip the halter over the nearest sheep's head, and there was a mad dash, all right. To the rear of the truck.

"Maybe you could pick one up and carry it off," I said, thinking of the cover of one of the angel books. It showed a barefoot angel carrying a lost lamb. "A small one."

Ben nodded. He handed me the halter and went up the ramp, moving slowly so he wouldn't scare them. "Shh, shh," he said softly to a little ewe. "I won't hurt you. Shh, shh."

The sheep didn't move. Ben knelt and got his arms under the front and back legs and hoisted the animal up. He started for the ramp.

The angel had clearly doped the sheep with chloroform before picking it up. The ewe kicked out with four hooves in four different directions, flailing madly and bringing its muzzle hard up against Ben's chin. He staggered and the ewe twisted itself around and kicked him in the stomach. Ben dropped it with a thud, and it dived into the middle of the truck, bleating hysterically.

The rest of the sheep followed. "Are you all right?" I said.

"No," he said, testing his jaw. "What happened to 'little lamb, so meek and mild'?"

"Blake had obviously never actually met a sheep," I said, helping him down the ramp and over to the water trough. "What now?"

He leaned against the water trough, breathing heavily. "Eventually they have to get thirsty," he said, gingerly touching his chin. "I say we wait 'em out."

Miguel bopped over to us. "I haven't got all day, you know!" he shouted over whatever was blaring in his headphones, and went back to the front of the truck.

"I'll go call Billy Ray," I said, and did. His cellular phone was out of range.

"Maybe if we sneak up on them with the halter," Ben said when I got back.

We tried that. Also getting behind them and pushing, threatening Miguel, and several long spells of leaning against the water trough, breathing hard.

"Well, there's certainly information diffusion going on," Ben said, nursing his arm. "They've all decided not to get off the truck."

Alicia came over. "I've got a profile of the optimum Niebnitz Grant candidate," she said to Ben, ignoring me. "And I've found another Niebnitz. An industrialist. Who made his fortune in ore refining *and* founded several charities. I'm looking into their committees' selection criteria." She added, still to Ben, "I want you to come see the profile."

"Go ahead," I said. "You obviously won't miss anything. I'll go try Billy Ray again."

I did. He said, "What you have to do is—" and went out of range again.

I went back out to the paddock. The sheep were out of the truck, grazing on the dry grass. "What did you do?" Ben said, coming up behind me.

"Nothing," I said. "Miguel must have gotten tired of waiting," but he was still up by the front of the truck, grooving to Groupthink or whatever it was he was listening to.

I looked at the sheep. They were grazing peacefully, wandering happily around the paddock as if they'd always belonged there. Even when Miguel, still wearing his headphones, revved up the truck and drove off, they didn't panic. One of them close to the fence looked up at me with a thoughtful, intelligent gaze.

This is going to work, I thought.

The sheep stared at me for a moment longer, dropped its head to graze, and promptly got it stuck in the fence.

qiao pai (1977–95) Chinese game fad inspired by the American card game bridge (a fad in the 1930s). Popularized by Deng Xiaoping, who learned to play in France, *qiao pai* quickly attracted over a million enthusiasts, who play mostly at work. Unlike American bridge, bidding is silent, players do not arrange their hands in order, and the game is extremely formalized. Superseded Ping-Pong.

Over the next few days it became apparent that there was almost no information diffusion in a flock of sheep. There were also hardly any fads.

"I want to watch them for a few days," Ben said. "We need to establish what their normal information diffusion patterns are."

We watched. The sheep grazed on the dry grass, took a step or two, grazed some more, walked a little farther, grazed some more. They would have looked almost like a pastoral painting if it hadn't been for their long, vacuous faces, and their wool.

I don't know who started the myth that sheep are fluffy and white. They were more the color of an old mop and just as matted with dirt.

They grazed some more. Periodically one of them would

leave off chewing and totter around the perimeter of the paddock, looking for a cliff to fall off of, and then go back to
grazing. Once one of them threw up. Some of them grazed
along the fence. When they got to the corner they stayed
there, unable to figure out how to turn it, and kept grazing,
eating the grass right down to the dirt. Then, for lack of better
ideas, they ate the dirt.

"Are you sure sheep are a higher mammal?" Ben asked,
leaning with his chin on his hands on the fence, watching
them.

"I'm so sorry," I said. "I had no idea sheep were this
stupid."

"Well, actually, a simple behavior structure may work to
our advantage," he said. "The problem with macaques is
they're smart. Their behavior's complicated, with a lot of
things going on simultaneously—dominance, familial interaction, grooming, communication, learning, attention structure.
There are so many factors operating simultaneously the problem is trying to separate the information diffusion from the
other behaviors. With fewer behaviors, it will be easier to see
the information diffusion."

If there is any, I thought, watching the sheep.

One of them walked a step, grazed, walked two more
steps, and then apparently forgot what it was doing and gazed
vacantly into space.

Flip slouched by, wearing a waitress uniform with red pip-
ing on the collar and "Don's Diner" embroidered in red on
the pocket, and carrying a paper.

"Did you get a job?" Ben asked hopefully.

Roll. Sigh. Toss. "No-o-o-o."

"Then why are you wearing a uniform?" I asked.

"It's *not* a uniform. It's a dress designed to *look* like a
uniform. Because of how I have to do all the work around

here. It's a *state*ment. You have to sign this," she said, handing me the paper and leaning over the gate. "Are these the sheep?"

The paper was a petition to ban smoking in the parking lot.

Ben said, "One person smoking one cigarette a day in a three-acre parking lot does not produce secondhand smoke in sufficient concentration to worry about."

Flip tossed her hair, her hair wraps swinging wildly. "*Not* secondhand smoke," she said disgustedly. "Air pol*lu*tion."

She slouched away, and we went back to observing. At least the lack of activity gave us plenty of time to set up our observation programs and review the literature.

There wasn't much. A biologist at William and Mary had observed a flock of five hundred and concluded that they had "a strong herd instinct," and a researcher in Indiana had identified five separate forms of sheep communication (the *baa*s were listed phonetically), but no one had done active learning experiments. They had just done what we were doing: watch them chew, totter, mill, and throw up.

We had a lot of time to talk about hair-bobbing and chaos theory. "The amazing thing is that chaotic systems don't always stay chaotic," Ben said, leaning on the gate. "Sometimes they spontaneously reorganize themselves into an orderly structure."

"They suddenly become less chaotic?" I said, wishing that would happen at HiTek.

"No, that's the thing. They become more and more chaotic, until they reach some sort of chaotic critical mass. When that happens, they spontaneously reorganize themselves at a higher equilibrium level. It's called self-organized criticality."

We seemed well on the way to it. Management issued memos, the sheep got their heads stuck in the fence, the gate, and under the feed dispenser, and Flip came periodically to hang on the gate between the paddock and the lab, flip the latch monotonously up and down, and look lovesick.

By the third day it was obvious the sheep weren't going to start any fads. Or learn how to push a button to get feed. Ben had set up the apparatus the morning after we got the sheep and demonstrated it several times, getting down on all fours and pressing his nose against the wide flat button. Feed pellets clattered down each time, and Ben stuck his head into the trough and made chewing noises. The sheep watched impassively.

"We're going to have to force one of them to do it," I said. We'd watched the videotapes from the day they arrived and seen how they'd gotten off the truck. The sheep had jostled and backed until one was finally pushed off onto the ramp. The others had immediately tumbled after it in a rush. "If we can teach one of them, we know the others will follow it."

Ben went resignedly to get the halter. "Which one?"

"Not that one," I said, pointing at the sheep that had thrown up. I looked at them, sizing them up for alertness and intelligence. There didn't appear to be much. "That one, I guess."

Ben nodded, and we started toward it with the halter. It chewed thoughtfully a moment and then bolted into the far corner. The entire flock followed, leaping over each other in their eagerness to reach the wall.

" 'And out of the houses the rats came tumbling,' " I murmured.

"Well, at least they're all in one corner," Ben said. "I should be able to get the halter on one of them."

Nope, although he was able to grab a handful of wool and hold on nearly halfway across the paddock.

"I think you're scaring them," Flip said from the gate. She

had been hanging on it half the morning, morosely flipping the latch up and down and telling us about Darrell the dentist.

"They're scaring me," Ben said, brushing off his corduroy pants, "so we're even."

"Maybe we should try coaxing them," I said. I squatted down. "Come here," I said in the childish voice people use with dogs. "Come on. I won't hurt you."

The sheep gazed at me from the corner, chewing impassively.

"What do shepherds do when they lead their flocks?" Ben asked.

I tried to remember from pictures. "I don't know. They just walk ahead of them, and the sheep follow them."

We tried that. We also tried sneaking up on both sides of a sheep and coming at the flock from the opposite side, on the off-chance they would run the other way and one of them would accidentally collide with the button.

"Maybe they don't like those feed pellet things," Flip said.

"She's right, you know," I said, and Ben stared at me in disbelief. "We need to know more about their eating habits and their abilities. I'll call Billy Ray and see what they do like."

I got Billy Ray's voice mail. "Press one if you want the ranchhouse, press two if you want the barn, press three if you want the sheep camp." Billy Ray wasn't at any of the three. He was on his way to Casper.

I went back to the lab, told Bennett and Flip I was going to the library, and drove in.

Flip's clone was at the desk, wearing a duct tape headband and an *i* brand.

"Do you have any books on sheep?" I asked her.

"How do you spell that?"

"With two *es*." She still looked blank. "S. H."

"The Sheik of Araby," she read from the screen, *"Middle-Eastern Sheiks and—"*

"*Sheep*," I said. "With a *p*."

"Oh." She typed it in, backspacing several times. "*The Mystery of the Missing Sheep*," she read. "*Six Silly Sheep Go Shopping, The Black Sheep Syndrome . . .*"

"Books *about* sheep," I said. "How to raise them and train them."

She rolled her eyes. "You *did*n't *say* that."

I finally managed to get a call number out of her and checked out *Sheep Raising for Fun and Profit; Tales of an Australian Shepherd;* Dorothy Sayers's *Nine Tailors*, which I seemed to remember had some sheep in it; *Sheep Management and Care;* and, remembering Billy Ray's sheep mange, *Common Sheep Diseases,* and took them up to be checked out.

"I show an overdue book for you," she said. "*Complete Words* by Robert Browning."

"*Works,*" I said. "*Complete Works.* We went through this last time. I checked it in."

"I don't show a return," she said. "I show a fine of sixteen fifty. It shows you checked it out last March. Books can't be checked out when outstanding fines exceed five dollars."

"I checked the book in," I said, and slapped down twenty dollars.

"Plus you have to pay the replacement cost of the book," she said. "That's fifty-five ninety-five."

I know when I am licked. I wrote her a check and took the books back to Ben, and we started through them.

They were not encouraging. "In hot weather sheep will bunch together and smother to death," *Sheep Raising for Fun, Etc.* said, and "Sheep occasionally roll over on their backs and aren't able to right themselves."

"Listen to this," Ben said. " 'When frightened, sheep may run into trees or other obstacles.' "

There was nothing about skills except "Keeping sheep inside a fence is a lot easier than getting them back in," but there was a lot of information about handling them that we could have used earlier.

You were never supposed to touch a sheep on the face or scratch it behind the ears, and the Australian shepherd advised ominously, "Throwing your hat on the ground and stomping on it doesn't do anything except ruin your hat."

" 'A sheep fears being trapped more than anything else,' " I read to Ben.

"Now you tell me," he said.

And some of the advice apparently wasn't all that reliable. "Sit quietly," *Sheep Management* said, "and the sheep will get curious and come to see what you're doing."

They didn't, but the Australian shepherd had a practical method for getting a sheep to go where you wanted.

" 'Get down on one knee beside the sheep,' " I read from the book.

Ben complied.

" 'Place one hand on dock,' " I read. "That's the tail area."

"On the tail?"

"No. Slightly to the rear of the hips."

Shirl came out of the lab onto the porch, lit a cigarette, and then came over to the fence to watch us.

" 'Place the other hand under the chin,' " I read. " 'When you hold the sheep this way, he can't twist away from you, and he can't go forward or back.' "

"So far so good," Ben said.

"Now, 'Hold the chin firmly and squeeze the dock gently to make the sheep go forward.' " I lowered the book and watched. "You stop it by pushing on the hand that's under the chin."

"Okay," Ben said, getting up off his knee. "Here goes."

He gave the woolly rear of the sheep a gentle squeeze. The sheep didn't move.

Shirl took a long, coughing drag on her cigarette and shook her head.

"What are we doing wrong?" Ben said.

"That depends," she said. "What are you trying to do?"

"Well, eventually I want to teach a sheep to push a button to get feed," he said. "For now I'd settle for getting a sheep on the same side of the paddock as the feed trough."

He had been holding on to the sheep and squeezing the whole time he'd been talking, but the sheep was apparently operating on some sort of delayed mechanism. It took two docile steps forward and began to buck.

"Don't let go of the chin," I said, which was easier said than done. We both grabbed for the neck. I dropped the book and got a handful of wool. Ben got kicked in the arm. The sheep gave a mighty lunge and took off for the middle of the flock.

"They do that," Shirl said, blowing smoke. "Whenever they've been separated from the flock, they dive straight back into the middle of it. Group instinct reasserting itself. Thinking for itself is too frightening."

We both went over to the fence. "You know about sheep?" Ben said.

She nodded, puffing on her cigarette. "I know they're the orneriest, stubbornest, dumbest critters on the planet."

"We already figured that out," Ben said.

"How do you know about sheep?" I asked.

"I was raised on a sheep ranch in Montana."

Ben gave a sigh of relief, and I said, "Can you tell us what to do? We can't get these sheep to do anything."

She took a long drag on her cigarette. "You need a bell-wether," she said.

"A bellwether?" Ben said. "What's that? A special kind of halter?"

She shook her head. "A leader."

"Like a sheepdog?" I said.

"No. A dog can harry and guide and keep the sheep in line, but it can't make them follow. A bellwether's a sheep."

"A special breed?" Ben asked.

"Nope. Same breed. Same sheep, only it's got something that makes the rest of the flock follow it. Usually it's an old ewe, and some people think it's something to do with hormones; other people think it's something in their looks. A teacher of mine said they're born with some kind of leadership ability."

"Attention structure," Ben said. "Dominant male monkeys have it."

"What do *you* think?" I said.

"Me?" she said, looking at the smoke from her cigarette twisting upward. "I think a bellwether's the same as any other sheep, only more so. A little hungrier, a little faster, a little greedier. It wants to get to the feed first, to shelter, to a mate, so it's always out there in front." She stopped to take a drag on her cigarette. "Not a lot. If it was a long way in front, the flock'd have to strike out on their own to follow, and that'd mean thinking for themselves. Just a little bit, so they don't even know they're being led. And the bellwether doesn't know it's leading."

She dropped her cigarette in the grass and stubbed it out. "If you teach a bellwether to push a button, the rest of the flock'll do it, too."

"Where can we get one?" Ben said eagerly.

"Where'd you get your sheep?" Shirl said. "The flock probably had one, and you just didn't get it in this batch. These weren't the whole flock, were they?"

"No," I said. "Billy Ray has two hundred head."

She nodded. "A flock that big almost always has a bellwether."

I looked at Ben. "I'll call Billy Ray," I said.

"Good idea," he said, but he seemed to have lost his enthusiasm.

"What's the matter?" I said. "Don't you think a bellwether's a good idea? Are you afraid it'll interfere with your experiment?"

"*What* experiment? No, no, it's a good idea. Attention structure and its effect on learning rate is one of the variables I wanted to study. Go ahead and call him."

"Okay," I said, and went into the lab. As I opened the door, the hall door slammed shut. I walked through the habitat and looked down the hall.

Flip, wearing overalls and Cerenkhov-blue-and-white saddle oxfords, was just disappearing into the stairwell. She must have been bringing us the mail. I was surprised she hadn't come out into the paddock and asked us if we thought she was captivating.

I went back in the lab. She'd left the mail on Ben's desk. Two packages for Dr. Ravenwood over in Physics, and a letter from Gina to Bell Laboratories.

flower child weddings (1968—75)

Rebellion fad made popular by people who didn't want to totally rebel against tradition and not get married at all. Performed in a meadow or on a mountaintop, the ceremony featured, "Feelings," played on a sitar and vows written by the participants with assistance from Kahlil Gibran. The bride generally wore flowers in her hair and no shoes. The groom wore a peace symbol and sideburns. Supplanted in the seventies by living together and lack of commitment.

Billy Ray brought the bellwether down himself. "I put it down in the paddock," he said when he came into the stats lab. "The gal down there said to just put it in with the rest of the flock."

He must mean Alicia. She'd spent all afternoon huddled with Ben, discussing the Niebnitz profile, which was why I'd come up to the stats lab to feed in twenties data. I wondered why Ben wasn't there.

"Pretty?" I said. "Corporate type? Wears a lot of pink?"

"The bellwether?" he said.

"No, the person you talked to. Dark hair? Clipboard?"

"Nope," he said. "Tattoo on her forehead."

"Brand," I said absently. "Maybe we'd better go check on the bellwether."

"She'll be fine," he said. "I brought her down myself so I could take you to that dinner we missed out on last week."

"Oh, good," I said. This would give me a chance to get some ideas of low-threshold skills we could teach the sheep. "I'll get my coat."

"Great," he said, beaming. "There's this great new place I want to take you to."

"Prairie?" I said.

"No, it's a Siberian restaurant. Siberian is supposed to be the hot new cuisine."

I hoped he meant *hot* in the sense of *warm*. It was freezing outside in the parking lot, and there was a bitter wind. I was glad Shirl didn't have to stand out there to have a cigarette.

Billy Ray led me to his truck and helped me in. As he started to pull out of the parking lot, I put my hand on his arm. "Wait," I said, remembering what Flip had done to my clippings. "Maybe we should check to make sure the bellwether's all right before we leave. What did she say exactly? The girl who was down there in the lab. She wasn't out in the paddock, was she?"

"Nope," he said. "I was looking for somebody to give the bellwether to, and she came in with some letters and said they were in Dr. Turnbull's lab and to just leave the bellwether in the paddock, so I did. She's fine. Got right off the truck and started grazing."

Which must mean she was really a bellwether. Things were looking up.

"She wasn't still there when you left, was she?" I said. "The girl, not the bellwether."

"Nope. She asked me whether I thought she had a good sense of humor, and when I said I didn't know, I hadn't heard her say anything funny, she kind of sighed and rolled her eyes and left."

"Good," I said. It was five-thirty already. Flip wouldn't have stayed a minute past five, and she usually left early, so the chances she would have come back to the lab to work mischief were practically nonexistent. And Ben was still there; he'd come back from Alicia's lab to check on things before he went home. If he wasn't too enamored of Alicia and the Niebnitz Grant to remember he had a flock of sheep.

"This place is great," Billy Ray said. "We'll have to stand in line an hour to get in."

"Sounds great," I said. "Let's go."

It was actually an hour and twenty minutes, and during the last half hour the wind picked up and it started to snow. Billy Ray gave me his sheepskin-lined jacket to put over my shoulders. He was wearing a band-collared shirt and cavalry pants. He'd let his hair grow out, and he had on yellow leather riding gloves. The Brad Pitt look. When I kept shivering, he let me wear the gloves, too.

"You'll love this place," he said. "Siberian food is supposed to be great. I'm really glad we were able to get together. There's something I've been wanting to talk to you about."

"I wanted to talk to you, too," I said through stiff lips. "What kinds of tricks can you teach sheep?"

"Tricks?" he said blankly. "Like what?"

"You know, like learning to associate a color with a treat or running a maze. Preferably something with a low ability threshold and a number of skill levels."

"Teach sheep?" he repeated. There was a long pause while the wind howled around us. "They're pretty good at getting out of fences they're supposed to stay inside of."

That wasn't exactly what I had in mind.

"I'll tell you what," he said. "I'll get on the Internet and see if anybody on there's ever taught a sheep a trick." He took off his hat, in spite of the snow, and turned it between his hands. "I told you I had something I wanted to talk to you about. I've had a lot of time to think lately, driving to Durango and everything, and I've been thinking a lot about the ranching life. It's a lonely life, out there on the range all the time, never seeing anybody, never going anywhere."

Except to Lodge Grass and Lander and Durango, I thought.

"And lately I've been wondering if it's all worth it and what am I doing it for. And I've been thinking about you."

"Barbara Rose," the Siberian waiter said.

"That's us," I said. I gave Billy Ray his coat and gloves back, and he put his hat on, and we followed the waiter to our table. It had a samovar in the middle of it, and I warmed my hands over it.

"I think I told you the other day I was feeling at loose ends and kind of dissatisfied," he said after we had our menus.

"Itch," I said.

"That's a good word for it. I've been itchy, all right, and while I was driving back from Lodgepole I finally figured out what I was itching for." He took my hand.

"What?" I said.

"You."

I yanked my hand back involuntarily, and he said, "Now, I know this is kind of a surprise to you. It was a surprise to me. I was driving through the Rockies, feeling out of sorts and like nothing mattered, and I thought, I'll call Sandy, and after I got done talking to you, I got to thinking, Maybe we should get married."

"Married?" I squeaked.

"Now I want to say right up front that whatever your answer is, you can have the sheep for as long as you want. No strings attached. And I know you've got a career that you don't want to give up. I've got that figured out. We wouldn't have to get married till after you've got this hair-bobbing thing done, and then we could set you up on the ranch with faxes and a modem and e-mail. You'd never even know you weren't right there at HiTek."

Except Flip wouldn't be there, I thought irrelevantly, or Alicia. And I wouldn't have to go to meetings and do sensitivity exercises. But married!

"Now, you don't have to give me your answer right away," Billy Ray went on. "Take all the time you want. I've had a couple of thousand miles to think about it. You can let me know after we have dessert. Till then, I'll leave you alone."

He picked up a red menu with a large Russian bear on it and began reading through it, and I sat and stared at him, trying to take this in. Married. He wanted me to marry him.

And, well, why not? He was a nice guy who was willing to drive hundreds of miles to see me, and I was, as I had told Alicia, thirty-one, and where was I going to meet anybody else? In the personals, with their athletic, caring NSs who weren't even willing to walk across the street to date somebody?

Billy Ray had been willing to drive all the way down from someplace on the off chance of taking me to dinner. And he'd loaned me a flock of sheep *and* a bellwether. And his gloves. Where was I going to meet anybody that nice? Nobody at HiTek was going to propose to me, that was for sure.

"What do you want?" Billy Ray asked me. "I think I'm going to have the potato dumplings."

I had borscht flavored with basil (which I hadn't remembered as being big in Siberian cuisine) and potato dumplings and tried to think. What did I want?

To find out where hair-bobbing came from, I thought, and knew that was about as likely as winning the Niebnitz Grant. In spite of Feynman's theory that working in a totally different field sparked scientific discovery, I was no closer to finding the source of fads than before. Maybe what I needed was to get away from HiTek altogether, out in the fresh air, on an isolated Wyoming ranch.

"Far from the madding crowd," I murmured.

"What?" Billy Ray said.

"Nothing," I said, and he went back to his dinner.

I watched him eat his dumplings. He really did look a little like Brad Pitt. He was awfully trendy, but maybe that would be an advantage for my project, and we wouldn't have to get married right away. He'd said I could wait until after I finished the project. And, unlike Flip's dentist, he wouldn't mind my being geographically incompatible while I worked on it.

Flip and her dentist, I thought, wondering uneasily if this was just another fad. That article had said marriage was in, and all the little girls were crazy for Romantic Bride Barbie. Lindsay's mother was thinking of getting married again in spite of that jerk Matt, Sarah was trying to talk Ted into proposing, and Bennett was letting Alicia pick out his ties. What if they were all part of a commitment fad?

I was being unfair to Billy Ray. He was in love with what was trendy, he might even stand in line in a blizzard for an hour and a half, but he wouldn't *marry* someone because marriage was in. And what if it was a trend? Fads aren't all bad. Look at recycling and the civil rights movement. And the waltz. And, anyway, what was wrong with going along with a trend once in a while?

"Time for dessert," Billy Ray said, looking at me from under the brim of his hat.

He motioned the waitress over, and she rattled off the usual suspects: crème brûlée, tiramisu, bread pudding.

"No chocolate cheesecake?" I said.

She rolled her eyes.

"What do you want?" Billy Ray said.

"Give me a minute," I said, breathing hard. "You go ahead."

Billy Ray smiled at the waitress. "I'll have the bread pudding," he said.

"Bread pudding?" I said.

The waitress said helpfully, "It's our most popular dessert."

"I thought you didn't like bread pudding," I said.

He looked up blankly. "When did I say that?"

"At that prairie cuisine place you took me to. The Kansas Rose. You had the tiramisu."

"Nobody eats tiramisu anymore," he said. "I love bread pudding."

virtual pets (fall 1994—spring 1996)—Japanese computer game fad featuring a programmed pet. The puppy or kitten grows when fed and played with, learns tricks (the dogs, presumably, not the cats), and runs away if neglected. Caused by the Japanese love of animals and an overpopulation problem that makes having pets impractical.

Ben met me in the parking lot the next morning. "Where's the bellwether?" he said.

"Isn't it in with the other sheep?" I scrambled out of the car. I *knew* I shouldn't have trusted Flip. "Billy Ray said he put it in the paddock."

"Well, if it's there, it looks just like all the other sheep."

He was right. It did. We did a quick count, and there was one more than usual, but which one was the bellwether was anybody's guess.

"What did it look like when your friend put it in the paddock?"

"I wasn't down here," I said, looking at the sheep, trying to detect one that looked different. "I knew I should have come down to check on it, but we were going out to dinner and—"

"Yeah," he said, cutting me off. "We'd better find Shirl."

Shirl was nowhere to be found. I looked in the copy room and in Supply, where Desiderata was examining her split ends, which were lying on the counter in front of her.

"What happened to you, Desiderata?" I said, looking at her hacked-off hair.

"I couldn't get the duct tape off," she said forlornly, holding up one of the still-wrapped hair strands. "It was worse than the rubber cement that time."

I winced. "Have you seen Shirl?"

"She's probably off smoking somewhere," she said disapprovingly. "Do you *know* how *bad* second-secondhand smoke is for you?"

"Almost as bad as duct tape," I said, and went down to Alicia's lab in case Shirl was feeding in stats for her.

She wasn't, but Alicia, wearing a po-mo pink silk blouse and palazzo pants, was. "*None* of the Niebnitz Grant winners was a smoker," she said when I asked her if she'd seen Shirl.

I thought about explaining that, given the percentage of nonsmokers in the general population and the tiny number of Niebnitz Grant recipients, the likelihood of their being non-smokers (or anything else) was statistically insignificant, but the bellwether was still unidentified.

"Do you know where Shirl might be?" I said.

"I sent her up to Management with a report," she said.

But she wasn't there either. I went back down to the lab. Bennett hadn't found her either. "We're on our own," he said.

"Okay," I said. "It's a bellwether, so it's a leader. So we put out some hay and see what happens."

We did.

Nothing happened. The sheep near Ben scattered when he forked the hay in and then went on grazing. One of them wandered over to the water trough and got its head stuck between it and the wall and stood there bleating.

"Maybe he brought the wrong sheep," Ben said.

"Do you have the videotapes from last night?" I said.

"Yeah," he said and brightened. "Your friend's bringing the bellwether will be on it."

It was. Billy Ray let down the back of the truck, and the bellwether trotted meekly down the ramp and into the midst of the flock, and it was a simple matter of following its progress frame by frame right up to the present moment.

Or it would have been, if Flip hadn't gotten in the way. She completely blocked the view of the flock for at least ten minutes, and when she finally moved off to the side, the flock was in a completely different configuration.

"She wanted to know if Billy Ray thought she had a sense of humor," I said.

"Of course," Ben said. "What now?"

"Back it up," I said. "And freeze-frame it just before the bellwether gets off the truck. Maybe it's got some distinguishing characteristics."

He rewound, and we stared at the frame. The bellwether looked exactly the same as the other ewes. If she had any distinguishing characteristics, they were visible only to sheep.

"It looks a little cross-eyed," Ben said finally, pointing at the screen. "See?"

We spent the next half hour working our way through the flock, taking ewes by the chin and looking into their eyes. They were all a little cross-eyed and so vacant-looking they should have had an *i* stamped on their long, dirty-white foreheads for *impenetrable*.

"There's got to be a better way to do this," I said after a deceptively scrawny ewe had mashed me against the fence and nearly broken both my legs. "Let's try the videotapes again."

"Last night's?"

"No, this morning's. And keep a tape running. I'll be right back."

I ran up to the stats lab, keeping an eye out for Shirl on

the way, but there was no sign of her. I grabbed the disk my vector programs were on and then started rummaging through my fad collection.

It had occurred to me on the way upstairs that if we did manage to identify the bellwether, we needed something to mark it with. I pulled out the length of po-mo pink ribbon I'd bought in Boulder and ran back down to the lab.

The sheep were gathered around the hay, chewing steadily on it with their large square teeth. "Did you see who led them to it?" I asked Ben.

He shook his head. "They all just seemed to gravitate toward it at once. Look." He switched on the videotape and showed me.

He was right. On the monitor, the sheep wandered aimlessly through the paddock, stopping to graze with every other step, paying no attention to each other or the hay, until, apparently by accident, they were all standing with their forefeet in the hay, taking casual mouthfuls.

"Okay," I said, sitting down at the computer. "Hook the tape in, and I'll see if I can isolate the bellwether. You're still taping?"

He nodded. "Continuous and backup."

"Good," I said. I rewound to ten frames before Ben had forked out the hay, froze the frame, and made a diagram of it, assigning a different colored point to each of the sheep, and did the same thing for the next twenty frames to establish a vector. Then I started experimenting to see how many frames I could skip without losing track of which sheep was which.

Forty. They grazed for a little over two minutes and then took an average of three steps before they stopped and ate some more. I started through at forty, lost track of three sheep within two tries, cut back to thirty, and worked my way forward.

When I had ten points for every sheep, I fed in an analysis program to calculate proximities and mean direction, and continued plotting vectors.

On the screen the movement was still random, determined by length of grass or wind direction or whatever it was in their tiny little thought processes that makes sheep move one way or the other.

There was one vector headed toward the hay, and I isolated it and traced it through the next hundred frames, but it was only a matted ewe determined to wedge itself into a corner. I went back to tracing all the vectors.

Still nothing on the screen, but in the numbers above it, a pattern started to emerge. Cerulean blue. I followed it forward, unconvinced. The sheep looked like she was grazing in a rough circle, but the proximities showed her moving erratically but steadily toward the hay.

I isolated her vector and watched her on the videotape. She looked completely ordinary and totally unaware of the hay. She walked a couple of steps, grazed, walked another step, turning slightly, grazed again, ending up always a little closer to the hay, and from halfway through the frames, the regression showed the rest of the flock following her.

I wanted to be sure. "Ben," I said. "Cover up the water trough and put a pan of water in the back gate. Wait, let me hook this up to the tape so I can trace it as it happens. Okay," I said after a minute. "Walk along the side so you don't block the camera."

I watched on the monitor as he maneuvered a sheet of plywood onto the trough, carried a pan out, and filled it with the hose, watching the sheep sharply to see if any of them noticed.

They didn't.

They stayed right by the hay. There was a brief flutter of activity as Ben carried the hose back and lifted the latch on the gate, and then the sheep went back to business as usual.

I tracked cerulean blue in real time, watching the numbers. "I've got her," I said to Bennett.

He came and looked over my shoulder. "Are you sure? She doesn't look too bright."

"If she was, the others wouldn't follow her," I said.

"I looked for you up*stairs*," Flip said, "but you weren't there."

"We're busy, Flip," I said without taking my eyes off the screen.

"I'll get the slip halter and a collar," Ben said. "You direct me."

"It'll just take a *min*ute," Flip said. "I want you to look at something."

"It'll have to wait," I said, my eyes still fixed on the screen. After a minute, Ben appeared in the picture, holding the collar and halter.

"Which one?" he shouted.

"Go left," I shouted back. "Three, no four sheep. Okay. Now toward the west wall."

"This is about Darrell, isn't it?" Flip said. "He was in a news*pa*per. Anybody who read it had a right to answer it."

"Left one more," I shouted. "No, not that one. The one in front of it. Okay, now, don't scare it. Put your hand on its hindquarters."

"Besides," Flip said, "it said 'sophisticated and elegant.' Scientists aren't *el*egant, except Dr. Turnbull."

"Careful," I shouted. "Don't spook it." I started out to help him.

Flip blocked my way. "All I want is for you to look at something. It'll only take a minute."

"Hurry," Ben called. "I can't hold her."

"I don't have a minute," I said and brushed past Flip, praying that Ben hadn't lost the bellwether. He still had her, but just barely. He was hanging on to her tail with both hands, and was still holding the halter and the collar. There was no way he could let go to give them to me. I pulled the ribbon out of my pocket, wrapped it around the bellwether's straining neck, and tied it in a knot. "Okay," I said, spreading my feet apart, "you can let go."

The rebound nearly knocked me down, and the bellwether immediately began pulling away from me and the not-nearly-strong-enough ribbon, but Ben was already slipping the halter on.

He handed it to me to hold and got the collar on, just as the ribbon gave way with a loud rip. He grabbed on to the halter, and we both held on like two kids flying a wayward kite. "The . . . collar's . . . on," he said, panting.

But you couldn't see it. It was completely swallowed up in the bellwether's thick wool. "Hold her a minute," I said, and looped what was left of the ribbon under the collar. "Hold still," I said, tying it in a big, floppy bow. "Po-mo pink is *the* color for fall." I adjusted the ends. "There, you're the height of fashion."

Apparently she agreed. She stopped struggling and stood still. Ben knelt beside me and took the halter off. "We make a great team," he said, grinning at me.

"We do," I said.

"*Well*," Flip said from the gate. She clicked the latch up and down. "Do you have a minute *now*?"

Ben rolled his eyes.

"Yes," I said, laughing. I stood up. "I have a minute. What is it you wanted me to look at?"

But it was obvious, now that I looked at her. She had dyed her hair—hank, hair wraps, even the fuzz of her shaved skull—a brilliant, bilious Cerenkhov blue.

"*Well?*" Flip said. "Do you think he'll like it?"

"I don't know, Flip," I said. "Dentists tend to be kind of conservative."

"I *know*," she said, rolling her eyes. "That's why I dyed it *blue*. Blue's a con*ser*vative color." She tossed her blue hank. "*You're* no help," she said, and stomped out.

I turned back to Ben and the bellwether, who was still standing perfectly still. "What next?"

Ben squatted next to the bellwether and took her chin in his hand. "We're going to teach you low-threshold skills," he said, "and you're going to teach your friends. Got it?"

The bellwether chewed thoughtfully.

"What would you suggest, Dr. Foster? Scrabble, Ping-Pong?" He turned back to the bellwether. "How'd you like to start a chain letter?"

"I think we'd better stick to pushing a button to open a feed trough," I said. "As you say, she doesn't look too bright."

He turned her head to one side and then the other, frowning. "She looks like Flip." He grinned at me. "All right, Trivial Pursuit it is. But first, I've got to go get some peanut butter. *Sheep Management and Care* says sheep love peanut butter," and left.

I tied a double knot in the bellwether's bow and then leaned on the gate and watched them. Their movements looked as random and directionless as ever. They grazed and took a step and grazed again, and so did she, indistinguishable from the rest of them except for her pallid pink bow, unnoticed and unnoticing. And leading.

She tore a piece of grass, chewed on it, took two steps, and stared blankly into space for a long minute, thinking about what? Having her nose pierced? The hot new exercise fad for fall?

"Here you are," Shirl said, carrying a stack of papers and

looking irate. "You're not engaged to that Billy Ray person, are you? Because if you are, that changes my entire—" She stopped. "Well, are you?"

"No," I said. "Who told you I was?"

"Flip," she said disgustedly. She set down the papers and lit a cigarette. "She told Sarah you were getting married and moving to Nevada."

"Wyoming," I said, "but I'm not."

"*Good,*" Shirl said, taking an emphatic drag on the cigarette. "You're a very talented scientist with a very bright future. With your ability, good things are going to happen to you very shortly, and you have no business throwing it all away."

"I'm not," I said, and made an effort to change the subject. "Did you want to see me about something?"

"Yes," she said, gesturing toward the paddock. "When the bellwether gets here, be sure you mark it before you put it in with the other sheep so you can tell which one it is. And there's an all-staff meeting tomorrow." She picked up the memos and handed one to me. "Two o'clock."

"Not *another* meeting," I said.

She stubbed out her cigarette and left, and I went back to leaning on the fence, watching the sheep. They were grazing peacefully, the bellwether in the middle of them, indistinguishable except for her pink bow.

I should move the feeding trough out to the paddock and check the circuits, so it'd be ready when Ben got back, I thought, but I went back in to the computer, traced vectors for a while, and then sat and looked at the screen, watching them move, watching the bellwether move among them, and thinking about Robert Browning and bobbed hair.

mood rings (1975)——

Jewelry fad consisting of a ring set with a large "stone" that was actually a temperature-sensitive liquid crystal. Mood rings supposedly reflected the wearer's mood and revealed his or her thoughts. Blue meant tranquillity; red meant crabbiness; black meant depression and doom. Since the ring actually responded to temperature, and after a while not even that, no one achieved the ideal "bliss" purple without a high fever, and everyone eventually sank into gloom and despair as their rings went permanently black. Superseded by Pet Rocks, which didn't respond to anything.

The bellwether could definitely make the flock do what she wanted. Getting the bellwether to do what we wanted her to do was another matter. She watched as we smeared peanut butter on the button she was supposed to push and then led the entire flock into a smothering jam-up in the back corner.

We tried again. Ben coaxed her with a rotten apple, which *Sheep Raising for Fun and Profit* had sworn they liked, and she trotted after him over to the trough. "Good girl," he said, and bent over to give her the apple, and she butted him smartly in the stomach and knocked the wind out of him.

We tried decayed lettuce next and then fresh broccoli,

neither of which produced any results—"At least it didn't butt you," I said—and then gave up for the night.

When I got to work the next morning with a bag full of cabbage and kiwi fruit *(Tales of an Australian Shepherd)*, Ben was smearing molasses on the button.

"Well, there's definitely been information diffusion," he said. "Three other sheep have already butted me this morning."

We led the bellwether over to the trough using the chin-rump-halter method and a squirt gun, which *Sheep Management and Care* had suggested. "It's supposed to keep them from butting."

It didn't.

I helped him up. *"Tales of an Australian Shepherd* said only the rams butt, not the ewes." I dusted him off. "It's enough to make you lose faith in literature."

"No," he said, holding his stomach. "The poet had it right. 'The sheep is a perilous beast.' "

On the fifth try we got her to lick the molasses. Pellets obligingly chattered into the trough. The bellwether gazed interestedly at it for a long minute, during which Ben looked at me and crossed his fingers, and then she bucked, catching me smartly on both ankles and making me let go of the halter. She dived headlong into the flock, scattering it wildly. One of the ewes ran straight into Ben's leg.

"Look on the bright side," I said, nursing my ankles. "There's an all-staff meeting at two o'clock."

Ben limped over and retrieved the halter, which had come off. "They're supposed to like peanuts."

The bellwether didn't like peanuts, or celery or hat-stomping. She did, however, like bolting and backing and trying to shake her collar off. At a quarter to one Ben looked at his watch and said, "Almost time for the meeting," and I didn't even contradict him.

I limped to the stats lab, washed off what lanolin and dirt I could and went up to the meeting, hoping Management would think I was making a sterling effort to dress down.

Sarah met me at the door of the cafeteria. "Isn't it exciting?" she said, sticking her left hand in my face. "Ted asked me to *marry* him!"

Commitment-Aversion Ted? I thought. The one who had severe intimacy issues and a naughty inner child?

"We went ice-climbing, and he hammered his piton in and said, 'Here, I know you've been wanting this,' and handed a ring to me. I didn't even make him. It was *so* romantic!

"Gina, look!" she said, charging toward her next victim. "Isn't it exciting?"

I went on into the cafeteria. Management was standing at the front of the room next to Flip. He was wearing jeans with a crease in them. She was wearing Cerenkhov blue toreador pants and a slouch hat that was pulled down over her ears. They were both wearing T-shirts with the letters SHAM across the front.

"Oh, no," I murmured, wondering what this would mean to our project, "not another acronym."

"Systemized Hierarchical Advancement Management," Ben said, sliding into the chair next to me. "It's the management style nine percent of the companies whose scientists won the Niebnitz Grant were using."

"Which translates to how many?"

"One. And they'd only been using it three days."

"Does this mean we'll have to reapply for funding for our project?"

He shook his head. "I asked Shirl. They don't have the new funding forms printed yet."

"We've got a lot on the agenda today," Management boomed, "so let's get started. First, there've been some problems with Supply, and to rectify that we've instituted a new streamlined procurement form. The workplace message facilitation director"—he nodded at Flip, who was holding a massive stack of binders—"will pass those out."

"The workplace message facilitation director?" I muttered.

"Just be glad they didn't make her a vice president."

"Secondly," Management said, "I've got some excellent news to share with you regarding the Niebnitz Grant. Dr. Alicia Turnbull has been working with us on a game plan that we're going to implement today. But first I want all of you to choose a partner—"

Ben grabbed my hand.

"—and stand facing each other."

We stood and I put my hands up, palms facing out. "If we have to say three things we like about sheep, I'm quitting."

"All right, HiTekkers," Management said, "now I want you to give your partners a big hug."

"The next big trend at HiTek will be sexual harassment," I said lightly, and Ben took me in his arms.

"Come on, now," Management said. "Not everybody's participating. *Big* hug."

Ben's arms in the faded plaid sleeves pulled me close, enfolded me. My hands, caught up in that palms-out silliness, went around his neck. My heart began to pound.

"A hug says, 'Thank you for working with me,' " Management said. "A hug says, 'I appreciate your personness.' "

My cheek was against Ben's ear. He smelled faintly of sheep. I could feel *his* heart pounding, the warmth of his breath on my neck. My breath caught, like a hiccuping engine, and stalled.

"All right now, HiTekkers," Management said. "I want you to look at your partner—still hugging, don't let go—and tell him or her how much he or she means to you."

Ben raised his head, his mouth grazing my hair, and

looked at me. His gray eyes, behind his thick glasses, were serious.

"I—" I said, and jerked out of his embrace.

"Where are you going?" Ben said.

"I have to—I just thought of something that ties into my hair-bobbing theory," I said desperately. "I've got to put it on the computer before I forget. About marathon dancing."

"Wait," he said, and grabbed my hand. "I thought marathon dancing wasn't until the thirties."

"It started in 1927," I said, and wrenched out of his grasp.

"But wasn't that still after the hair-bobbing craze?" he said, but I was already out the door and halfway up the stairs.

hair wreaths (1870—90) Ghoulish Victorian handicraft fad in which the hair of a deceased loved one (or assortment of loved ones, preferably with different-colored hair) was made into flowers. The hair (obtained somehow or other) was braided and woven into bouquets and wreaths, and placed under a glass dome, or framed and hung on the wall. Supplanted by the suffrage movement, croquet, and Elinor Glyn. The hair wreath fad may have been a contributing factor in the hair-bobbing fad of the 1920s.

Significant breakthroughs have been triggered by all sorts of things—apples, frog legs, photographic plates, finches—but mine must be the only one ever triggered by one of Management's idiotic sensitivity exercises.

I didn't stop till I was inside the stats lab. I hugged my arms to my chest and leaned against the door, panting and murmuring, over and over again, "Stupid, stupid, stupid."

I was supposed to be such an expert at spotting trends, but it had taken me weeks to see where this one was leading. And all that time I'd thought it was his immunity to fads I was interested in. I'd taken notes on his cloth sneakers and ties. I'd even seriously considered Billy Ray's proposal. And all that time—

There was somebody coming down the hall. I hastily sat down in front of the computer, pulled up a program, and sat there, staring blindly at it.

"Busy?" Gina said, coming in.

"Yes," I said.

"Oh," and her expression plainly said, "You don't look busy." "I couldn't find you after the meeting. I took a bathroom break right before they started the sensitivity exercise, and when I got back, you were gone. I just wanted to bring you the list of toy stores I've already tried so you don't waste your time on them."

"Right," I said. "I'll go this weekend."

"Oh, no hurry. Bethany's birthday isn't for another two weeks, but it makes me kind of nervous that Toys "R" Us was out of it. That's where Chelsea's mother found the one for Brittany, and she said it was the only place she could find one." She frowned. "Are you okay? You look like somebody who got sent to her room for a time-out."

A time-out. You'll just have to sit here quietly until you can get control of your feelings, young lady.

"I'm fine," I said. "I should have listened to your advice and taken a bathroom break, that's all."

She nodded. "Those sensitivity exercises'll do you in. Well, I'll let you get back to work. Or whatever." She patted me on the shoulder.

"And I'll deliver Romantic Bride Barbie. You don't have to worry. I'll find it," I said, and started sorting blindly through a stack of clippings.

As soon as she was gone I shut the door, and then went back and sat down at the computer and stared at the screen.

The file I'd called up was my hair-bobbing model. It sat there, with its crisscrossing colored lines and that anomalous cluster in Marydale, Ohio, like a reproach.

How could I hope to understand what had motivated

women to cut their hair seventy years ago when I didn't even understand what motivated me?

I hadn't even had a clue. Until Ben put his arms around me and pulled me close, I'd honestly thought I was trying to salvage his project because I couldn't stand Flip. I'd even thought the reason I was irritated with Alicia was because she was trying to produce science-on-demand. And all the time—

I heard a noise in the hall and put my hands on the keyboard. I needed to look busy so no one else would come talk to me.

I stared at the model, with its intersecting patterns, its crisscrossing curves, every event impacting on every other, iterating and reiterating and leading inevitably to an outcome.

Like my downfall. And maybe what I should be doing was drawing that, graphing the events and interactions that had led me to this pass. I called up the paintbox and an empty file and started trying to reconstruct the whole debacle.

I had borrowed Billy Ray's sheep. No, it had started before that, with Management and GRIM. Management had ordered a new funding form, and Ben's had gotten lost, and I had suggested we work together. And Management had said yes because they wanted one of HiTek's scientists to win the Niebnitz Grant.

I started drawing in the connecting lines, from Management's meetings to the funding forms to Shirl, the new assistant, who had brought me extra copies of the missing pages, which I'd taken down to Ben, to Alicia, who wanted to collaborate with Bennett to win the Niebnitz Grant. And back to Management and GRIM. And Flip.

"You left the meeting *early*," Flip said reprovingly, opening the door. She still had on the pulled-down hat, but she'd abandoned the SHAM T-shirt and was wearing a see-through dress over a bodysuit that appeared to be made of Cerenkhov blue duct tape.

"You didn't get your streamlined supply procurement processing form," she said, and handed me a binder. "And I *want*ed to ask you a question."

"I'm busy, Flip," I said.

"It'll *on*ly take a *min*ute," she said. "I know you're still mad about my answering the personal ad, but you're the only one I can ask. Desiderata and Shirl are both really nevved at me."

I *wonder* why, I thought. "I am really busy, Flip."

"It'll only take a *min*ute." She pulled a stool over next to the computer and perched on it. "How far should somebody go when they're really unbalanced about somebody?"

This was just what I needed, to discuss the sex life of a person with a pierced nose and duct tape underwear.

"I mean, if you thought you'd never see him again, do you think it's stupid to do something really swarb?"

I had talked Ben into combining our projects. I had borrowed a flock of sheep. Stupid, stupid, stupid.

"It's about my hair," she said, and pulled off her hat. "I cut it off."

She certainly had. Her hair was chopped to within an inch of her blue scalp. For a second I thought she'd had the same problem with the duct tape as Desiderata, but her flipping hank had been hacked off, too. She looked like a very cold plucked chicken.

I felt a sudden pang of empathy for her, in love with a dentist, of all people, who didn't know she existed, who was probably already engaged.

"So what I wondered," she said, "was whether it looks okay like this or whether I should add another brand." She pointed to her right temple, just below the scalped area.

"Of what?" I said faintly.

She sighed. "Of a strip of duct tape, of course."

Of course.

"I think it depends on how you're going to let your hair grow out," I said, hoping she was going to.

Apparently she was, because she put her hat back on again and said, "So you don't, then? Think it would be stupid?"

She apparently didn't expect an answer because she was already halfway out the door.

"Flip," I said, "would you do me a favor? Would you go down to Bio and tell Dr. O'Reilly I'm leaving early, and I'll talk to him tomorrow?"

"Bio is clear on the other side of the building," she said, outraged. "Anyway, I doubt if he's down there. When I left the meeting, he was talking to Dr. Turnbull. *Like* always. I bet he wishes he'd had her for a partner for that hug thing."

"I'm really busy, Flip," I said, and started typing to prove it. Flip. This was all Flip's fault. She had lost Bennett's funding forms *and* stolen my personal ads, which is why I'd been in the copy room when Bennett came in.

"Did you know Dr. Patton got engaged?" Flip said conversationally. "To that guy who didn't want to get married?"

"Yes," I said.

"I'll bet Dr. O'Reilly and Dr. Turnbull get married pretty soon."

I continued to type doggedly, and after a while Flip got bored and slouched off, but I didn't stop. I hadn't been kidding when I said this mess was all Flip's fault. She hadn't just lost the funding forms and stolen the personals. She had started the whole thing. If she hadn't delivered Dr. Turnbull's package to me in the first place, I would never even have met Ben. I never even got down to Bio, and at that first meeting he'd been clear on the other side of the room.

I kept adding lines, tracing the interconnecting events. She had thrown away six weeks' worth of research and stolen my stapler. And she'd left pages out of the funding forms. I'd had to take the missing pages to Ben. The prints of her Mary

Janes and backless clogs were all over the place, making mischief.

She was like some Iago. Or some evil guardian angel. "Always there, right there beside you, wherever you go," was what *Angels, Angels Everywhere* had said. And it was true. She was everywhere, like some awful anti-Pippa, wandering past unsuspecting windows and wreaking havoc wherever she went.

I added more lines. Flip raising her hand and getting an assistant, Flip spearheading the antismoking campaign that had made me suggest the paddock to Shirl, who had told us about the bellwether. Flip getting me depressed that day in Boulder. If it hadn't been for her talking about feeling itch, I would never have gone out with Billy Ray, I would never have known Targhees were sheep, and I would never have come up with the idea of borrowing them.

And Ben would be off somewhere in France, studying chaos theory, I thought bleakly. I knew none of this was Flip's fault. I was the one who'd made up excuses to see Ben, to talk to him, from that very first day when I'd followed him out on the porch.

Flip wasn't the source. She might have precipitated things, but the outcome was my fault. I had been following the oldest trend of all. Right over the cliff.

Flip was back, standing and looking interestedly over my shoulder.

"I'm still busy, Flip," I said.

She tossed her nonexistent hank. "Dr. O'Reilly left. I bet he went out on a date with Dr. Turnbull."

A ghastly unlosable guardian angel. "Don't you have someplace you need to go?" I said.

"That's what I *came* to tell you," she said. "Bye."

And left. I pondered the screen, wondering how to graph that little encounter, but she was already back.

"Are there hats in Texas?" she said.

"Ten-gallon ones," I said.

She left again, this time apparently for good. I added a few more lines to my graph, and then just sat there and stared at the crisscrossing curves, the neatly plotted regressions.

"Seven o'clock," Gina said, sticking her head in the door. She had her coat on. "You can come out of time-out now."

I smiled. "Thanks, Mom," I said, but I didn't leave. I waited till I was sure everybody was gone and then went down and hung over the gate, watching the sheep as they moved and grazed and moved again, occasionally bleating, occasionally lost, impelled by bellwethers they didn't recognize, by instincts they didn't know they had.

kewpies (1909–15) —— Doll fad derived from illustrated poems in the *Ladies' Home Journal*. Kewpie dolls looked like rosy-cheeked cherubs, with round tummies and a yellow curl on top of their heads. Wildly popular with adults and little girls, kewpies appeared as paper dolls, salt shakers, greeting cards, wedding cake decorations, and prizes at county fairs.

For the next two days I kept clear of the lab and Ben, straightening up *my* lab and entering miles of data about mah-jongg and Lindbergh's flight across the Atlantic.

This is ridiculous, I told myself on Thursday. You're not Peyton. You have to see him sometime. Grow up.

But when I got down to the lab, Alicia was there, leaning over the gate. Ben had the bellwether by her po-mo pink bow and was explaining the principle of attention structure. He was wearing his blue tie.

"This has *real* possibilities," Alicia was saying. "Thirty-one percent of all projects the Niebnitz Grant recipients were working on at the time of the award were cross-discipline collaborations. The thing is getting the *right* collaboration. The committee is obviously going for gender balance, which you're okay on, but chaos theory and statistics are both math-based disciplines. You need a biologist."

"Do you need me?" I said.

They both looked up.

"If not, I have some research I need to do at the library."

"No, go ahead," Ben said. "The bellwether's not in the mood to learn anything this morning." He rubbed his knee. "She's already butted me twice. While you're at the library, see if they've got anything on how to get a leader to follow."

"I will," I said, and started down the hall.

"Wait," Ben said, sprinting to catch up with me. "I wanted to talk to you. Did you have a breakthrough? With the dance marathon thing?"

Yes, I thought, looking at him forlornly. A breakthrough. "No," I said. "I thought there was a connection, but there wasn't," and I went to Boulder to look for Romantic Bride Barbie.

Gina had given me a list of toy stores, with the ones she'd already tried crossed off, which didn't leave all that many. I started at the top, determined to work my way down.

I had only thought I understood the Barbie fad. Not even Brittany's birthday party had prepared me for what I actually found.

There were Fashion Bright Barbies, Costume Ball Barbies, Bubble Angel Barbies, Sunflower Barbies, and even a Locket Surprise Barbie, whose plastic chest opened up to dispense lip gloss and rouge. There were multicultural Barbies, Barbies that lit up, remote-control Barbies, Barbies whose hair you could bob.

Barbie had a Porsche, a Jaguar, a Corvette, a Mustang, a speedboat, an RV, and a horse. Also a beauty bath, a Fun Fridge, a health spa, and a McDonald's. Not to mention the Barbie jewelry boxes, lunchboxes, workout tapes, audiotapes, videotapes, and pink nail polish.

But no Romantic Bride Barbie. The Toy Palace had Country Bride Barbie, with a pink-checked gingham sash and a bouquet of daisies. Toys "R" Us had a Dream Wedding Barbie and Barbie's Wedding Fantasy, both of which I seriously considered in spite of Gina's injunctions.

The Cabbage Patch had four full aisles of Barbies and a clerk with an *i* stamped on her forehead. "We have Troll Barbie," she said, when I asked her about Romantic Bride. "And Pocahontas."

I made it through four toy stores and three discount stores and then drove over to the Caffe Krakatoa to see if there were any Barbies listed in the personals.

It was now calling itself Kepler's Quark, a bad sign.

"Don't tell me. You don't have latte anymore," I said to the waiter, who was wearing a black turtleneck, black jeans, and sunglasses.

"Caffeine's bad for you," he said, handing me the menu, which had grown to ten pages. "I'd suggest a smart drink."

"Isn't that an oxymoron?" I said. "Believing a beverage can increase your IQ?"

He tossed his head, revealing an *i* on his forehead.

Of course.

"Smart drinks are nonalcoholic beverages with neurotransmitters to enhance memory and alertness and increase brain function," he said. "I'd suggest the Brain Blast, which increases your math skills, or the Get Up and Van Gogh, which enhances your artistic ability."

"I'll have the Reality Check," I said, hoping it would enhance my ability to face facts.

I tried reading the personals, but they were too depressing: "To the blonde who eats lunch every day at Jane's Java Joint, you don't know me but I'm hopelessly in love with you. Please reply."

I switched to the articles.

A "harmonic bonding" therapist was offering duct tape soul alignments.

Two men in New York City had been arrested for operating the hot new fad, a "smoking speakeasy."

Po-mo pink had fizzled as a fad. A fashion designer was quoted as saying, "There's no accounting for the public's taste."

Truer words, I thought, and it was time I faced that, too. I was never going to discover the source of the hair-bobbing fad, no matter how much data I fed into my computer model. No matter how many different colored lines I drew.

Because it didn't have anything to do with suffrage or World War I or the weather. And even if I could ask Bernice and Irene and the rest of them why they'd done it, it still wouldn't help. Because they wouldn't know.

They were as benighted and blind as I had been, moved by feelings they weren't aware of, by forces they didn't understand. Right straight into the river.

My smart drink came. It was chartreuse, a color that had been a fad in the late twenties. "What's in it?" I said.

He sighed, a heavy sigh like someone out of Dostoyevsky. "Tyrosine, L-phenylalanine, and synergistic cofactors," he said. "And pineapple juice."

I took a sip of it. I didn't feel any smarter. "Why did you get your forehead branded?" I said.

Apparently he hadn't finished his smart drink. He stared at me blankly.

"Your *i* brand?" I said, pointing at it. "Why did you decide to have it done?"

"*Every*body has them," he said, and slouched off.

I wondered if he had gotten the brand to please his girlfriend or if he was rebelling against anti-intellectualism or his parents, or in love with somebody who didn't know he was alive.

I sipped my drink and kept reading. I didn't feel any smarter. Bantam Books had paid an eight-figure advance for

Getting in Touch with Your Inner Fairy Godmother. Cerenkhov blue was the "cool/hot" color for winter, and men and women were smoking cigars in L.A., inspired by Rush Limbaugh or David Letterman or forces they didn't understand. Like sheep. Like rats.

None of which solved the problem of how I was going to go on working with Bennett. Or of where I was going to find Romantic Bride Barbie.

I went over to the library and checked out *Anna Karenina* and *Cyrano de Bergerac* and got the Denver phone book from the reference section. I copied down all the toy stores that weren't on Gina's list and all the department and discount stores, explained to Flip's clone that I had already paid the fine on Browning's *Complete Works*, and set out again, marking off stores as I went.

I eventually found Romantic Bride Barbie at a Target in Aurora—wedged in behind Barbie's Horse Stable Club—and took it up to the checkout.

The clerk was trying to make change for the man in front of me.

"It's eighteen seventy-eight," she said.

"I *know*," the man said. "I gave you a twenty-dollar bill and then after you rang it up as eighteen seventy-eight, I gave you three cents. You owe me a dollar and a quarter."

She flipped her hair back, irritably, revealing an *i*.

Give up, I thought. It's no use.

"The register says one twenty-two," she said.

"I *know*," he said. "That's why I gave you the three cents. Twenty-two plus three makes a quarter."

"A quarter of *what*?"

I set Romantic Bride Barbie on the end of the counter. I read the tabloid headlines and looked at the impulse items on the rack next to the counter. Duct tape in several widths, and bubble packs of Barbie high heels in assorted colors.

"All *right*, fine," the man said. "Give me back the three cents and give me one twenty-two."

I picked up a pack of high heels. "New! Cerenkhov blue," it read. I set it down next to the duct tape and as I did, I felt a strange sensation, as if I were on the verge of something important, like the final side of a Rubik's cube clicking into place.

"This doesn't have a price on it," the checkout clerk said. She was holding Romantic Bride Barbie. "I can't sell anything that doesn't have a price on it."

"It's thirty-eight ninety-nine," I said. "The manager said to ring it up under Miscellaneous."

"Oh," she said, and rang it up.

This is a fad I could actually learn to like, I thought, smiling at her *i*. Forewarned is forearmed.

"That'll be forty-one thirty-three," she said. I stood there, wallet in hand, looking at the boxes of crayons, trying to recapture the feeling I'd had. Something about Cerenkhov blue, and duct tape, or—

Whatever it was, it was gone. I hoped it hadn't been the cure for cholera.

"Forty-one thirty-*three*," the clerk said.

I carefully counted out the exact change and left with Romantic Bride Barbie. On the way out, I stepped on something and looked down. It was a penny. Farther on there were two more. They looked like they had been flung down with some force.

prohibition (1895—january 16, 1920)———Aversion fad against alcohol fueled by the Women's Christian Temperance Union, Carry Nation's saloon-smashing, and the sad effects of alcoholism. Schoolchildren were urged to "sign the pledge" and women to swear not to touch lips that had touched liquor. The movement gained impetus and political support all through the early 1900s, with party candidates drinking toasts with glasses of water and several states voting to go dry, and finally culminated in the Volstead Act. Died out as soon as Prohibition was enacted. Replaced by bootleggers, speakeasies, bathtub gin, hip flasks, organized crime, and Repeal.

Gina couldn't believe I'd found Romantic Bride Barbie. She hugged me twice. "You're wonderful. You're a miracle worker!"

"Not quite," I said, trying to smile. "I don't seem to be having any luck finding the source of hair-bobbing."

"Speaking of which," she said, still admiring Romantic Bride Barbie, "Dr. O'Reilly was up here before, looking for you. He looked worried."

What's Flip lost now? I wondered, the bellwether? and started down to Bio. Halfway there, I ran into Ben. He grabbed my arm. "We were supposed to be in Management's office ten minutes ago."

"Why? What's this about?" I asked, trying to keep up. "Are we in trouble?"

Well, of course we were in trouble. The only time anybody got to see the inside of Management's office, Staff Input notwithstanding, was when they were getting transferred to Supply. Or having their funding cut.

"I hope it isn't the animal-rights activists," Ben said, coming to a stop outside Management's door. "Do you think I should have worn a jacket?"

"No," I said, remembering his jackets. "Maybe it's something minor. Maybe we didn't dress down enough."

The secretary in the outer office told us to go right in. "It's not something minor," Ben whispered, and reached for the doorknob.

"Maybe we're not in trouble," I said. "Maybe Management's going to commend us for cross-disciplinary cooperation."

He opened the door. Management was standing behind his desk with his arms folded.

"I don't think so," Ben murmured, and we went in.

Management told us to sit down, another bad sign. One of SHAM's Eight Efficiency Enhancers was "Holding meetings standing up encourages succinctness."

We sat.

Management remained standing. "An extremely serious matter has come to my attention concerning you and your project."

It is the animal-rights activists, I thought, and braced myself for what he was going to say next.

"The assistant workplace message facilitator was observed smoking in the area of the animal compound. She says she had permission to do so. Is that true?"

Smoking. This was about Shirl's smoking.

"Who gave her this permission?" Management demanded.

"I did," we both said. "It was my idea," I said. "I asked Dr. O'Reilly if it was all right."

"Are you aware that the HiTek building is a smoke-free zone?"

"It was outside," I said, and then remembered Berkeley. "I didn't think she should have to stand out in the middle of a blizzard to smoke."

"I didn't either," Ben said. "She didn't smoke inside. Just in the paddock."

Management looked even grimmer. "Are you aware of HiTek's guidelines for live-animal research?"

"Yes," Ben said, looking bewildered. "We followed the—"

"Live animals are required to have a healthy environment," Management said. "Are you aware of the dangers of atmospheric carcinogens, the FDA's report on the dangers of secondhand smoke? It can cause lung cancer, emphysema, high blood pressure and heart attacks."

Ben looked even more confused. "She didn't smoke anywhere near us, and it was outside. It—"

"Live animals are required to have a *healthy* environment," Management said. "Would you call smoke a healthy environment?"

Never underestimate the power of an aversion trend, I thought. The last one in this country ended in wholesale accusations of communist leanings, ruined reputations, destroyed careers.

" '. . . out of the houses the rats came tumbling,' " I murmured.

"What?" Management said, glaring at me.

"Nothing."

"Do you know what the effects of secondhand smoke on sheep are?" Management said.

No, I thought, and you don't either. You're just following the flock.

"Your blatant disregard for the health of the sheep has clearly made the project ineligible for serious consideration as a grant contender."

"She only smoked one cigarette a day," Ben said. "The compound where the sheep are is a hundred feet by eighty. The density of the smoke from a single cigarette would be less than one part per billion."

Give it up, Ben, I thought. Aversion trends have nothing to do with scientific logic, and we've not only exposed sheep to secondhand smoke, HiTek thinks we've jeopardized its chances of winning its heart's desire, the Niebnitz Grant.

I looked at Management. HiTek's actually going to fire somebody, I thought, and it's us.

I was wrong.

"Dr. Foster, you were the one who obtained the sheep, weren't you?"

"Yes," I said, resisting the urge to add "sir." "From a rancher in Wyoming."

"And is he aware that you intended exposing his sheep to harmful carcinogens?"

"No, but he won't object," I said, and then remembered the bread pudding. I had never asked him his views on smoking, but I knew what they were: whatever everyone else thought.

"As I recall, this project was your idea, too, Dr. Foster," Management said. "It was your idea to use sheep, in *spite* of Management's objections."

"She was only trying to help me save my project," Ben said, but Management wasn't listening.

"Dr. O'Reilly," he said, "this unfortunate situation is

clearly not your fault. The project will have to be terminated, I'm afraid, but Dr. Turnbull is in need of a colleague for the project she is working on, and she specifically requested you."

"*What* project?" Ben said.

"That hasn't been decided yet," Management said. "She is looking into several possibilities. Whatever, I'm sure it will be an excellent project to be involved with. We feel it has a seventy-eight percent chance of winning the Niebnitz Grant." He turned back to me. "Dr. Foster, I'll hold you responsible for returning the sheep to their owner immediately."

The secretary came in. "I'm sorry to interrupt, Mr.—"

"A reprimand will be placed in your file, Dr. Foster," Management said, ignoring her, "and there will be a serious reexamination of your project at the next funding allocation period. In the meantime—"

"Sir, you need to come out here," the secretary said.

"I'm in the middle of a meeting," Management cut in. "I want a full report detailing your progress in trends research," he said to me.

"Now wait a minute," Ben said. "Dr. Foster was only—"

The secretary said, "*Excuse me*, Mr.—"

"What *is* it, Ms. Shepard?" Management said.

"The sheep—"

"Has the owner called to complain?" he said, shooting me a venomous glance.

"No, sir. It's the sheep. They're in the hall."

5. main channel

God's in his heaven—
All's right with the world.

robert browning

dancing mania (1374)

Northern European religious fad in which people danced uncontrollably for hours. They formed circles in streets and churches and leaped, screamed, and rolled on the ground, often shouting that they were possessed by demons and begging said demons to stop tormenting them. Caused by nervous hysteria and/or the wearing of pointed shoes.

The idea that chaos and significant scientific breakthroughs are connected was first proposed by Henri Poincaré, who had been unable to forget putting his foot on the omnibus step and having it all come clear. The pattern of his discovery, he told the Société de Psychologie, was one of unexpected insight arising out of frustration, confusion, and mental chaos.

Other chaos theorists have explained Poincaré's experience as the result of the conjunction of two distinct frames of reference. The chaotic circumstances—Poincaré's frustration with the problem, his insomnia, the distractions of packing for a trip, the change of scenery—created a far-from-equilibrium situation in which unconnected ideas shifted into new and startling conjunctions with each other and tiny events could have enormous consequences. Until chaos could be crystallized into a higher order of equilibrium by the simple act of stepping onto a bus. Or into a flock of sheep.

They weren't in the hall. They were in the outer office and on their way into Management's white-carpeted inner sanctum. The secretary flattened herself against the wall to let them pass, clutching her steno pad to her chest.

"Wait!" Management said, putting his hands up as if doing a sensitivity exercise. "You cannot come in here!"

Ben dived to head off the lead ewe, which must not have been the bellwether, because even though he got it stopped at the door and held it there, pushing against its shoulders like a football tight end, the other sheep simply swarmed past it and into Management's office. And maybe I had misjudged them and they did have brains. They had unerringly headed straight for the part of the building where they could do the most damage.

They did it, tracking in an amount of dirt I wouldn't have thought their little cloven hooves could carry, leaving a long smear of dirt-laden lanolin on the white walls and Management's secretary as they brushed past them.

Ben was still struggling with the ewe, which was eager to join the flock, now heading straight for Management's polished teak desk.

"Endangering the welfare of live animals," Management said, clambering up on top of it. "Providing inadequate project supervision."

The sheep were circling the desk like Indians riding around a wagon train.

"Failing to institute proper security measures!" Management said.

"Facilitating potential," I murmured, trying to get them moving in another direction, any direction.

"These animals should not be in here!" Management shouted from the top of his desk.

The same idea had apparently occurred to the sheep. They set up a pitiful bleating all at once, opening their mouths in a continuous, deafening *baa*.

I looked sharply at the sheep, trying to spot where the bleating had originated, but it had seemed to come from everywhere at once. Like hair-bobbing.

"Did you hear where the bleating started?" I shouted to Ben, who let go of the ewe, and the sheep were suddenly on the move again, milling randomly through the office and toward the door to the secretary's hall.

"Where are they going?" Ben said.

Management had clambered down off his desk and was shouting warnings again, looking slightly more dressed-down than before. "HiTek will not tolerate employee sabotage! If either of you or that *smoker* let these sheep out on purpose—"

"We didn't," Ben said, trying to get to the door. "They must have gotten out by themselves," and I had a sudden image of Flip leaning on the paddock gate, flipping the latch up and down, up and down.

Ben made it to the door as the last two sheep were squeezing through, bleating frantically at the thought of being left behind.

But once in the hall they began milling aimlessly around, looking lost but immovable.

"We have to find the bellwether," I said. I began to work my way through them, searching for the pink ribbon.

There was a yelp from the end of the hall and a "Blast you, you brainless critter!" It was Shirl, her arms full of papers. "Get out of my way, you fool animal!" she shouted. "How did you get—" She stopped short at the sight of the hallful of sheep. "Who let them out?"

"Flip," I said, feeling around a ewe's neck for the ribbon.

"She can't have," Shirl said, wading toward me through the sheep. "She's not here."

"What do you mean she's not here?" I said. Two ewes pushed past me on either side and nearly knocked me down.

"She quit," Shirl said, swatting at the one on the left with her papers. "Three days ago."

"I don't care," I said, pushing at the other one. "Somehow, somewhere, Flip is behind this. She's behind everything."

The sheep surged suddenly down the hall toward Personnel. "Where are they going now?" Ben said.

"They have no idea," I said. "Behold the American public."

Management emerged from his office, Dockers in disarray. "This sort of behavior is obviously a side effect of nicotine!"

"We have to find the bellwether," I said. "It's the key."

Ben stopped. He looked at me. "The key," he said.

Management bellowed, "When I find out who's causing this—this chaos—"

"Chaos," Ben said, almost to himself. "The key's the bellwether."

"Yes," I said. "It's the only way we can get them back to Bio. You start at this end, and I'll take the other end. Okay?"

He didn't answer me. He stood, transfixed, while the sheep milled around him, his mouth half open, his eyes squinting behind his Coke-bottle glasses. "A bellwether," he said softly.

"Yes, the bellwether," I said, and it took a long moment for his eyes to focus on me. "Find the bellwether. Think pink," and I started for the end of the hall. "Shirl, run down to the lab and get a halter and lead." Something suddenly struck me. "Did you say Flip quit?"

Shirl nodded. "That dentist she met in the personals. He moved, and she followed him. So they could be geographically compatible." She went back down the hall in the direction of Bio.

The sheep were in the stairwell, milling frightenedly at the edge of the top stair, and it was too bad it wasn't a cliff. Maybe they'd still fall down it and break their necks—but no such luck. They clambered lightly down a flight and into the hall to Stats. I ran back upstairs. "They're heading for Stats!" I shouted to Ben.

He wasn't there. I ran back down the stairs and stopped halfway. In a corner on the floor, thoroughly trampled and very dirty, was the pink ribbon. Wonderful, I thought, and looked up to see Alicia Turnbull glaring at me. "Dr. *Foster*," she said disapprovingly.

"Don't tell me," I said. "None of the Niebnitz Grant winners were ever involved in livestock stampedes."

"Where is Dr. O'Reilly?" she demanded.

"I don't know," I said. I picked up the draggled ribbon. "I don't know where the bellwether is either. Or what sort of project will win the Niebnitz Grant. I do, however, have a good idea what those sheep are doing to Stats at this very minute, so if you'll excuse me—" I said, and pushed past her out of the stairwell and into the hall.

At least they can't do any damage in my lab, I thought, hoping the rest of the doors were shut.

The flock was still in the hall, so they must be. Gina was at the far end, coming out of the stats lab.

"Time for a bathroom break," she said as soon as she saw them, and ducked through a door.

I started through the sheep, leaning down to lift up their chins and look into their vacant faces for an expression that looked slightly cross-eyed or halfway intelligent.

The door opened again. "There's one in the bathroom," Gina said. She edged her way down the hall toward where I was gazing into the sheeps' eyes.

They all looked cross-eyed. I peered anxiously into their long faces, into their vacant eyes, that were born to have an *i* branded between them.

"There'd better not be one in my office," Gina said, and opened her door.

"Shut your door!" I said, but too late. A fat ewe was already through it. "*Shut* it," I said again, and she did.

The rest of the sheep congregated outside her door, milling and *baa*ing, desperately seeking someone to tell them what to do, where to go. Which must mean the ewe in Gina's office was the bellwether.

"Keep it there!" I shouted through the door. The ribbon wasn't strong enough for a leash, but I had a Davy Crockett jump rope that might be. I started for my lab, wondering what had happened to Ben. Probably Alicia had found him and was telling him about her Niebnitz sure thing.

There was a shriek from Gina's office, and her door opened.

"Don't—" I shouted. The ewe dived through the door and into the midst of the flock like a card disappearing into a deck. "Did you see where she went, Gina?"

"No," she said tightly. "I didn't." She was clutching a battered pink box. A torn white net ruffle trailed from one corner. "Look what that *sheep* did to Romantic Wedding Barbie!" she said, holding up a lock of brunette hair. "It was the last one in Boulder."

"In the greater Denver area," I said, and went into the stats lab.

All I need now is Flip, I thought, and was amazed she wasn't there in the stats lab, having quit or not. A sheep was, munching thoughtfully on a disk. I grabbed it out of her mouth, or most of it, pried her large square teeth apart, fished out the remaining piece, and looked squarely into her slightly crossed eyes.

"Listen to me," I said, holding on to her jaw. "I've had all I can take for one day. I've lost my job, I've lost the only person I've ever met who doesn't act like a sheep, I don't know where fads come from and I'm never going to find out, and I've *had* it. I want you to follow me, and I want you to follow me now." I threw the pieces of disk on the floor and turned and walked out of my lab.

And she must have been the bellwether, because she trotted after me all the way down two flights into Bio, and through the lab to the paddock, just like Mary and her little lamb. And the rest of the flock followed, wagging their tails behind them.

ostrich plumes (1890—1913)——Edwardian fashion fad inspired by Charles Darwin and related public interest in natural history. The curling plumes were dyed all colors and worn in the hair, on hats, fans, and even feather dusters. Related fads included trimming hats and dresses with lizards, spiders, toads, and centipedes. As a result of the fad, ostriches were hunted into extinction in Egypt, North Africa, and the Middle East. Recurred in 1960s with minidresses, wigs, and capes of ostrich plumes dyed neon orange and hot pink.

I called Billy Ray to come pick the sheep up.

"I'll send Miguel down with the truck right away," he said. "I'd come myself, but I've got to go down to New Mexico and talk to this rancher about ostriches."

"Ostriches," I said.

"They're the latest thing. Reba's raising fifty of them on a spread outside Gallup, and ostrich steak's selling like gangbusters. Lower in cholesterol than chicken and tastes better."

One of the sheep had gotten itself stuck in the corner of the fence again. It stood there, looking blankly at the fence post like it had no idea how it had gotten there.

"Plus you can sell the feathers and tan the skin for purses

and boots," Billy Ray said. "Reba says they're going to be *the* livestock of the nineties."

The sheep butted its head against the post a couple of times and then gave up and stood there, bleating, a nice object lesson.

"I'm sorry the sheep thing didn't work out," Billy Ray said.

Me too, I thought. "You're getting out of range," I said. "I can't hear you," and hung up.

You can learn a lot from sheep. I went over to the corner and put my hands under its chin and on its rump. "You have to turn around," I said. "You have to go in another direction."

I dragged it around to face the other way. It immediately began to graze.

"You have to admit it's no use and go try something else," I said, and went back into the lab. Shirl was there. "Where's Dr. O'Reilly?" I said.

"He was in talking to Dr. Turnbull a minute ago," she said.

"Good," I said, and went back up to my stats lab to write up my report for Management.

"Sandra Foster: Project Report," I typed on a disk the ewe hadn't eaten.

Project goals:

1. Determine what triggers fads.
2. Determine the source of the Nile.

Project results:

1. Not found. Pied Piper may have something to do with it, for all I know. Or Italy.
2. Found. Lake Victoria.

Suggestions for further research:

1. Eliminate acronyms.
2. Eliminate meetings.
3. Study effect of antismoking fad on ability to think clearly.
4. Read Browning. And Dickens. And all the other classics.

I printed it out, and then gathered up my coat and non-wallet-on-a-string and went up to see Management.

Shirl was there, running a carpet cleaning machine. Management was dusting off his desk, which had been pushed against one corner.

"Don't step on the carpet," he said when I came in. "It's wet."

I walked squishily over to his desk. "The sheep are all in the paddock," I said over the sucking sound of the carpet steamer. "I've arranged for them to be sent back." I handed him my report.

"What's this?" he said.

"You said you wanted to reevaluate my project's goals," I said. "So do I."

"What's this?" he said, scowling at it. "Pied *Pip*er?"

"By Robert Browning," I said. "You know the story. Piper is hired to free Hamelin of rats, does so, but the town refuses to pay him. 'And as for our Corporation—shocking.' "

Management reared up behind his desk. "Are you threatening me, Dr. Foster?"

"No," I said, surprised. " 'Insulted by a lazy ribald?' " I quoted, " 'You threaten us, fellow? Do your worst,/Blow your pipe until you burst.' You should read more poetry. You can learn a lot from it. Do you have a library card?"

"A library—?" Management said, looking apoplectic.

"I'm not threatening you," I said. "Why would I? I didn't get rid of any rats *or* find out what causes hair-bobbing. I couldn't even locate a piper."

I stopped, thinking about that, and just like the night before, standing in line at Target with the late Romantic Bride Barbie, I felt like I was on the verge of something significant.

"Are you calling HiTek a rat?" Management said, and I waved him away impatiently, trying to focus on my elusive thought. A piper.

"Are you saying—" Management bellowed, and it was gone.

"I'm saying you hired me for the wrong reason. You shouldn't be looking for the secret to making people follow fads, you should be looking for the secret to making them think for themselves. Because that's what science is all about. And because the next fad may be the dangerous one, and you'll find it out with the rest of the flock on your way over the cliff. And no, I don't need a security escort back to my lab," I said, opening my purse so he could see inside. "I'm leaving. 'Up the Hill-side yonder, through the morning,'" and I squished my way back across the carpet. "Bye, Shirl," I called to her, "you can come smoke at my house anytime," and I went out to my car and drove to the library.

rubik's cube (1980—81)

Game fad involving a cube made up of smaller cubes of different colors that could be rotated to form different combinations. The object of the game (which more than a hundred million people tried to solve) was to twist the sides of the cube until each side was a solid color. The fad's skill threshold was somewhat too high—as witness the dozens of puzzle-help books published—and the fad died out with many people never having solved it even once.

Lorraine was back. "Do you want *Your Guardian Angel Can Change Your Life*?" she asked me. She was wearing a fairy godmother sweatshirt and sparkly magic wand earrings. "It came in, and so did your book on hair-bobbing."

"I don't want it," I said. "I don't know what caused it, and I don't care."

"We found that book on Browning. You had checked it in after all. Our media organization assistant shelved it with the cookbooks."

See, I told myself—walking over to Kepler's Quark and giving my first name to a waitress with chopped-off hair and a waitress uniform that probably wasn't a uniform—things are looking up already. They found Browning, you never have to read the personals again, and Flip can't slouch in here to ruin your day and stick you with the check.

The waitress seated me at a table by the window. See, I told myself again, she didn't seat you at the communal table. She isn't wearing duct tape. Definitely looking up.

But it didn't feel like it. It felt like I was out of a job. It felt like I was in love with somebody who didn't love me back.

He's totally fashion-impaired, I told myself. Look on the bright side. You no longer have to worry about what caused hair-bobbing. Which was a good thing, because I was pretty much out of ideas.

"Hi," Ben said, sitting down across from me.

"What are you doing here?" I said as soon as I was able to. "Shouldn't you be at work?"

"I quit," he said.

"You quit? Why? I thought you were going to work on Dr. Turnbull's project."

"You mean Alicia's statistically-thought-out, science-on-demand, sure-to-win-the-Niebnitz-Grant project? It's too late. The Niebnitz Grant has already been awarded."

He didn't look upset about it. He didn't look like somebody who'd just quit his job. He looked containedly excited, his eyes jubilant behind the Coke bottles. He's going to tell me he's engaged to Alicia, I thought.

"Who won it?" I said, to stop him. "The Niebnitz Grant. A thirty-eight-year-old designed experimenter from west of the Mississippi?"

Ben motioned the waitress over and said, "What have you got to drink that's not coffee?"

The waitress rolled her eyes. "There's our new drink. The Chinatasse. It's the latest thing."

"Two Chinatasses," he said, and I waited for the waitress to quiz him on whole vs. skim, white vs. brown, Beijing vs.

Guangzhou, but Chinatasses apparently had a lower skill threshold than caffè latte. The waitress slouched off, and Ben said, "This came for you," and handed me a letter.

"How did you know where to find me?" I said, looking at the envelope. It was blank except for my name.

"Flip told me," he said.

"I thought she was gone."

"She told me a while back. She said you hung out here a lot. I came here three or four times, hoping I'd run into you, but I never did. She said you came here looking for guys in the personals."

"Flip," I said, shaking my head. "I was reading them for trends research. I wasn't trying . . . you did?"

He nodded, no longer jubilant. His gray eyes were serious behind the Coke-bottle glasses. "I stopped coming a couple of weeks ago because Flip told me you were engaged to the sheep guy."

"Ostrich," I said. "Flip told me you were crazy about Alicia, that that's why you wanted to work with her."

"Well, at least now we know what the *i* on her forehead stands for. *Interfering*. I don't want to work with Alicia. I want to work with you."

"I'm not engaged to the sheep guy," I said. I thought of something. "Why did you buy that Cerenkhov blue tie?"

"To impress you. Flip told me you'd never go out with me unless I got some new clothes, and this awful blue was the only thing I could find in the stores." He looked sheepish. "I also took out an ad in the personals."

"You did? What did it say?"

"Insecure, ill-dressed chaos theorist desires intelligent, insightful, incandescent trends researcher. Must be SC."

"SC?"

"Scientifically compatible." He grinned. "People do crazy things when they're in love."

"Like borrow a flock of sheep to keep somebody from losing their grant?"

The waitress plunked down two glasses in front of us, spilling Chinatasse everywhere.

"We need those to go," Ben said.

The waitress sighed loudly and stomped off with them.

"If we're going to be working together," Ben said to me, "we'd better get started."

"Wait a minute," I said. "We both quit, remember?"

"Well, the thing is, HiTek wants us back."

"They do?"

"All is forgiven." He nodded. "They say we can have anything we need—lab space, assistants, computers."

"But what about the sheep and the secondhand smoke?"

"Open the letter."

I did.

"Read it."

I did. "I don't understand," I said.

I turned the letter over. There wasn't anything on the back. I looked at the envelope again. It still only had my name on it. I looked at Ben, who looked jubilant again. "I don't understand," I said again.

"Me neither," he said. "Alicia was there when I opened mine. She had to recalculate all her percentages."

I read the letter again. "We won the Niebnitz Grant?"

"We won the Niebnitz Grant."

"But . . . we aren't . . . we don't . . ."

"Well, that's the thing," he said, leaning across the table and, finally, taking my hand. "I had this idea. You know how I told you chaotic systems could be predicted by measuring all the variables and calculating the iteration? Well, I think Verhoest was right after all. There *is* another factor at work. But it's not an outside factor. It's something already in the system. Remember how Shirl said the bellwether was the same as the other sheep, only a little greedier, a little faster, a little ahead? What if—"

"—instead of butterflies, there's a bellwether in chaotic systems?" I said.

"Exactly." He was holding both my hands now. "And it doesn't look any different from the other variables in the system, but it's the trigger for the iteration, it's the catalyst, it's—"

"Pippa," I said, clutching his hands. "There's this poem, *Pippa Passes*, by—"

"Browning," he said. "She sings at people's windows—"

"And changes their lives, and they never even see her. If you were making a computer model of the village of Asolo, you wouldn't even put her in it, but she's—"

"—the variable that sets the butterfly's wings in motion, the force behind the iteration, the trigger behind the trigger, the factor that causes—"

"—women to bob their hair in Hong Kong."

"Exactly. The trigger that causes your fads. The—"

"—source of the Nile."

The waitress came back with the same two glasses. "We don't have cups to go. It pollutes the environment." She set the glasses down and stomped off again.

"Like Flip," Ben said, thinking about it. "She misdelivered the package, and that's how I met you."

"Among other things," I said, and felt that feeling again of being on the verge of something, of the Rubik's cube starting to turn.

"Let's go," Ben said. "I want to see what happens when I add the bellwether into my chaos theory data."

"Wait—I want to drink my Chinatasse, in case it's the next fad. And there's something else . . . You didn't give HiTek our decision yet, did you, about staying?"

He shook his head. "I thought you'd want to be there."

"Good," I said. "Don't tell them no yet. There's something I want to check on."

"Okay. I'll meet you back at HiTek in a few minutes then," he said. "Okay?" and went out.

"Umm," I said, trying to catch the thought I'd had before. Something about trains, or was it buses? And something the waitress had said.

I took a thoughtful sip of the Chinatasse, and if I needed a sign that chaos was reattaining equilibrium at a new and higher level, this was it. It was the Earth Mother's wonderful spiced iced tea.

Which should inspire me if anything could. But I couldn't capture the thought. The idea that I should have gone back with Ben kept intruding, and that, except for that sensitivity exercise, and some incidental hand-holding, he had never touched me.

And apparently there was some kind of feedback loop operating in our system because he was back and pushing past the waitress, who wanted to write his name down, and through the tables and pulling me to my feet. And kissing me.

"Okay," he said, when we pulled apart.

"Okay," I said breathlessly.

"Wow!" the waitress said. "Did you meet him in the personals?"

"No," I said, wishing she would shut up and that Ben would kiss me again. "Through Flip."

"We were introduced by a bellwether," Ben said, putting his arms around me again.

"*Wow!*" the waitress said.

couéism (1923)—— Psychology fad inspired by Dr. Emile Coué, a French psychologist and the author of *Self-Mastery by Auto-Suggestion.* Coué's method of self-improvement consisted of knotting a piece of string and reciting over and over, "Every day in every way, I am getting better and better." Died out when it became apparent no one was.

Scientific breakthroughs have been triggered by the most minor of events: the sight of bathwater rising, the movement of a breeze, the pressure of a foot on a step. I had never heard of one being triggered by a kiss, though.

But it was a kiss that had the full weight of five weeks of chaotic turbulence behind it, shifting patterns of thought out of their accustomed positions, stirring up the variables, separating and mixing them again into new conjunctions, new possibilities. And when Ben had put his arms around me, it had been like the discovery of penicillin and the benzene ring and the Big Bang all rolled into one. Eureka to the tenth power. Like coming to the source of the Nile.

"This FLIP thing, where you met him," the waitress was saying, "is it like a recovery group?"

"*Discovery*," I said, staring transfixed after Ben, wondering how I could have been so blind. It was all so clear: what triggered fads and how scientific breakthroughs happen and why we had won the Niebnitz Grant.

"Can anybody join this FLIP?" the waitress said. "I'm already in a latte recovery group, but there aren't any cute guys in it."

"I need my check," I said, fishing a twenty out of my purse and handing it to her so I could go back to HiTek and get all this on the computer.

"He already paid," she said, trying to hand me back the twenty.

"Keep it," I said, and grinned at her as something else hit me. "We're rich. We won the Niebnitz Grant!"

I hurried back to HiTek and up to the stats lab, and called up my hair-bobbing model.

Suppose fads were a form of self-organized criticality arising out of the chaotic system of the popular culture. And suppose that, like other chaotic systems, they were influenced by a bellwether. The independence of women, Irene Castle, outdoor sports, rebellion against the war, all of those would simply be variables in the system. They would require a catalyst, a butterfly to set them in motion.

I focused in on the bump in Marydale, Ohio. Suppose that wasn't a statistical anomaly. Suppose there'd been a girl in Marydale, Ohio, a girl just like everybody else, with flapping galoshes and rouged knees, indistinguishable from the rest of the flock, only a little greedier, a little faster, a little hungrier. A little ahead of the flock. A girl who had had a crush on a dentist on the other side of town and had walked into the barbershop and, with no idea she was starting a fad, that she was crystallizing chaos into criticality, told the barber to cut off her hair.

I called up the rest of the twenties data and asked for geographical breakdowns, and there was the anomaly again, for rolled-down stockings and the crossword puzzle, right over Marydale. And for the shimmy, even though the dance had originated in New York. But it hadn't become a fad until a bobbed-haired girl in Marydale, Ohio, had picked it up. A girl like Flip. A butterfly. A bellwether. The source of the Nile.

I called up the paintbox and traced the course of events at HiTek again, from Flip's misdelivering Dr. Turnbull's package to her fiddling with the latch on the gate, but this time I also fed in *Led On by Fate* and the bread pudding, Management's sensitivity exercises, the duct tape, Elaine's exercises, Shirl's smoking, Sarah's boyfriend, Romantic Bride Barbie, and the various skill levels of caffè latte.

All the variables I could think of and every one of Flip's actions, irrelevant or not, all of them feeding back into the system, adding turbulence, and leading not, as I'd thought after the sensitivity exercise, to disaster, but to the Niebnitz Grant, to love and to geographic compatibility and the source of hair-bobbing. To a new, higher state of equilibrium.

Flip had felt itch, and as a result I had told Billy Ray I'd go out with him, and he'd said he felt itch, too, and told me about the sheep, which I'd thought of when Flip lost Ben's funding form.

Flip. Her footprints, like Barbie's sharp little high heels, like the echoes of Pippa's voice, were all over the crime scene. She had told Ben I was engaged to Billy Ray, she had failed to copy pages 29 through 41, she had taught the bellwether to open the gate, she had told Management about Shirl's smoking, upping the level of chaos each time, mixing and separating the variables.

The screen filled with lines. I connected them, feeding in the iteration equations, and the lines became a tangle, the tangle a knot. The lost stapler, Browning's "Pied Piper," Billy Ray's cellular phone, po-mo pink. Flip had circulated a non-smoking petition and Shirl had ended up out in the parking lot in a blizzard and I took her down to Ben's lab and she watched Ben and me struggle with the sheep and said, "You need a bellwether."

The screen went dark, layer on layer of events feeding back into each other, and then sprang suddenly into a new design. A beautiful, elaborate structure, vivid with radical red and cerulean blue.

Self-organized criticality. Scientific breakthrough.

I sat and looked at it for a while, marveling at its simplicity and thinking about Flip. I had been wrong. The *i* on her forehead didn't stand for *incompetence* or *itch*. Or even *influence*. It stood for *inspiration*. And she was Pippa after all, only instead of singing she was stirring up the variables, upping the level of chaos with every petition and misdelivered package until the system went critical.

I also thought about penicillin and Alexander Fleming, with his crowded, too-small lab, heaped with piles of moldy petri dishes. The institute he worked in had been right in the middle of chaos—half a block from Paddington Station on a noisy street. Add in the vacation and the August heat and the new research assistant he had had to make room for, and all those tributary details like his father and the rifle team. And water polo. At school he'd been on a team that played a water polo match against St. Mary's Hospital. Three years later, when he was getting ready to go to medical school, he picked St. Mary's because he remembered the name.

Add in that, and the soot and the open window of the lab above, and you had a real mess. Or did you?

David Wilson had called the discovery of penicillin "Quite one of the luckiest accidents that ever occurred in nature." But was it? Or was it a scientific discovery waiting to happen, a system so chaotic that all it would take to push it over the edge into self-organized criticality was a spore, drifting in through an open window like Pippa's song?

Poincaré had believed creative thought was a process of inducing inner chaos to achieve a higher level of equilibrium. But did it have to be inner?

I saved everything to disk, stuck it in my pocket, and went down to Bio.

"I need to know something," I asked Ben. "Your bellwether chaos theory. Did you figure it out little by little or did it hit you all at once?"

He frowned. "Both. I'd been thinking about Verhoest and his X factor, and that maybe he was right, and I started trying to think what form another factor might take."

"And that's when the apple hit you on the head?"

He shook his head. "Alicia came in to tell me her research showed the next Niebnitz Grant recipient would be a radio astronomer and that Management had called another meeting, and then we had the sensitivity hug and for a couple of days after that all I could think about was you and how you were engaged to that cowboy."

"Ostrich rancher," I corrected. "For a couple of weeks, at least. So the ideas were in there percolating, but do you remember what it was that put it all together?"

"You did," he said. "The sheep were milling around in the hall outside of Management, and you said, 'Flip did this. I know it,' and Shirl said she wasn't there, and you said, 'I don't care. Somehow she's behind this.' And I thought, No, she isn't. The bellwether is. And I remembered Flip leaning on the paddock gate, flipping the lock up and down, and I thought, The bellwether must have learned how to open it from her, and led the rest of the sheep into this chaos.

"And it hit me, just like that. Bellwethers cause chaos. They're the unseen factor."

"I *knew* it," I said. "I have to go find something. Just what I thought. You're wonderful. Be right back." I kissed him for inspiration, and went to find Flip.

I had forgotten she'd quit. "Three days ago," Elaine in Personnel said. She was wearing a pair of Cerenkhov blue Rollerblades. "In-in-line skating," she said, raising her leg to demonstrate. "It gives a much better full-body workout than wall-walking, and it helps you get around the office faster. Did you hear about Sarah and her boyfriend?"

"They broke up?" I said.

"No. They got *married!"*

I pondered the implications of that. "Did Flip leave a forwarding address?" I asked. "Or say where she was going?"

She shook her head. "She said to give her check to Desiderata down in Supply and she'd send it on to her."

"Can I see her file?"

"Personnel records are confidential," she said, suddenly businesslike.

"Call Management and ask them," I said. "Tell them it's me."

She did. "Management said to give you anything you want," she said bemusedly, hanging up. "Do you want the whole file?"

"Just her previous work record."

She skated over to the file cabinet, got it, and skated over to me, executing a neat toe stop.

It was what I'd expected. Flip had worked at a coffeehouse in Seattle, and before that at a Burger King in L.A. "Thanks," I said, handing it back to her, and then thought of something else. "Let me see her file a minute." I opened it and glanced at the top line, where it said "full name, last, first, middle initial."

"Orliotti," it said. "Philippa J."

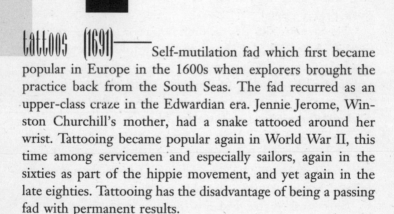

tattoos (1691) Self-mutilation fad which first became popular in Europe in the 1600s when explorers brought the practice back from the South Seas. The fad recurred as an upper-class craze in the Edwardian era. Jennie Jerome, Winston Churchill's mother, had a snake tattooed around her wrist. Tattooing became popular again in World War II, this time among servicemen and especially sailors, again in the sixties as part of the hippie movement, and yet again in the late eighties. Tattooing has the disadvantage of being a passing fad with permanent results.

I wrote down Flip's last name and made a note to find out her grandmother's maiden name and check to see if she was living anywhere near Marydale, Ohio, in 1921, and went down to Supply.

Desiderata couldn't find Flip's forwarding address. "She said she was going to someplace in Arizona," Desiderata said, looking in among the erasers. "Albuquerque, I think."

"Albuquerque is in New Mexico," I said.

"Oh," she said, frowning. "Then maybe it was Fort Worth. Wherever he went."

"Who?"

She rolled her eyes. "The *dentist* guy."

Of course. He had particularly specified geographic compatibility.

"Maybe she told Shirl," Desiderata said, rummaging through the pencils.

"I thought Shirl got fired," I said, "for smoking in the paddock."

"Hunh-unh," Desiderata said. "She quit. She said she was only going to stay till they hired a new workplace message facilitation director, and they did that this morning, so maybe she's already gone."

She wasn't. She was in the copy room, fixing the copy machine before she left, but Flip hadn't told Shirl where she was going either. "She mentioned something about this Darrell moving his practice to Prescott," Shirl said, leaning over the paper feed. "I heard you and Dr. O'Reilly won the Niebnitz Grant. That's wonderful."

"It is," I said, watching her yank a jammed sheet of paper out of the feed with her fingers. There were no signs of nicotine stains on them. "It's too bad I don't know who gives the grant. I had something I wanted to tell them."

Shirl pushed the feed into position and closed the lid. "I'm sure the committee wants to remain anonymous."

"If it is a committee," I said. "Committees are terrible at keeping secrets, and even Dr. Turnbull wasn't able to find out anything. I think it's one person."

"One very rich person," she said, her voice no longer raspy.

"Right. Somebody circumstantially predisposed to wealth, who thinks for herself and wants other people to, too. When did you quit smoking?"

"Flip converted me," she said. "Filthy habit. Hazardous to your health."

"Umm," I said. "Somebody extremely competent—"

"Speaking of which," she said, "have you run into Flip's

replacement yet? It'll make you glad you don't work here any-more. I didn't think it was possible to hire somebody worse than Flip, but Management's succeeded."

"Somebody extremely competent," I repeated, looking steadily at her, "who travels around the country like Diogenes, looking for scientists with circumstantial predispositions to scientific discovery. Somebody no one would suspect."

"Interesting theory," Shirl said dismissively, centering the paper on the glass plate. "What was it you wanted to tell this person? If he or she is incognito, he or she probably doesn't want to be thanked." She hit a button and started to lower the lid.

"Oh, I wasn't going to thank her," I said. "I was going to tell her she's going about things all wrong."

The copy light flashed blindingly. Shirl blinked. "You're saying the Niebnitz people picked the wrong winners?"

"It's not the people you choose. It's the grant itself. A million dollars means the scientist can quit his job, get a lab all his own, pursue his work in complete peace and quiet."

"And that's a bad thing?"

"Maybe. Look at Einstein. He discovered relativity while he was working in a dinky patent office, full of papers and contraptions. When he tried to work at home, it was even worse. Wet laundry hanging everywhere, a baby squalling on one knee, his first wife yelling at him."

"And those seem like ideal working conditions to you?"

"Maybe. What if instead of being hindrances, the noise and the damp laundry and the cramped apartment all com-bined to create a situation in which new ideas could coalesce?" I held up two fingers. "Only *two* of the winners of the Nieb-nitz Grant have gone on to make significant discoveries. Why?"

"Scientific discoveries can't be produced on demand. They take long years of painstaking work—"

"And luck. And serendipity. A breeze blowing Galvani's frog legs against a railing and closing a circuit, a hand getting in the way of cathode rays, an apple falling. Fleming. Penzias and Wilson. Kekulé. Scientific breakthroughs involve combining ideas no one thought to connect before, seeing connections nobody saw before. Chaotic systems create feedback loops that tend to randomize the elements of the system, displace them, shake them around so they're next to elements they've never come in contact with before. Chaotic systems tend to increase in chaos, but not always. Sometimes they restabilize into a new level of order."

"Archimedes," Shirl said.

"And Poincaré. And Roentgen. All of their ideas came out of chaotic situations, not peace and quiet. And if a chaotic situation could be *induced* instead of us having to just wait for it to happen . . . It's just an idea, but it accounts for why dozens of scientists could experiment with electrically discharged gases and never discover X rays. It accounts for why so many discoveries are made by scientists outside their field. Which is why you specified 'circumstantially predisposed,' why you choose people working outside their field, because you knew how it worked, even if you didn't know why. Of course it's still just an idea. But it fits with Bennett's theory of the bellwether effect. I'll need a lot more data, and—"

Shirl was smiling a not-at-all-pinched smile at me. "And you still think I'm going about it all wrong?" she said. She leaned over to pull the copy out of the machine. "Interesting theory," she said, picking up a stack of papers. "If I ever run into whoever it is that gives the Niebnitz Grant, I'll be sure to pass it on." She started out the door.

"Goodbye," I said, and kissed her on her leathery cheek.

"What was that for?" she grumbled, rubbing at her cheek with her hand.

"Fixing the copy machine," I said. "Oh, by the way," I called after her. "Who's the Niebnitz Grant named after?"

"Alfred Taylor Niebnitz," she said without turning her head. "My high school physics teacher."

ouija board (1917–18) — Psychic game fad that purports to tell the future. Players push a planchette around a board with letters and numbers, spelling out answers to questions. Originated either in Maryland in the 1880s with C. W. Kennard or William and Isaac Fuld or in Europe in the 1850s, but did not become a fad until America entered World War I. Recurs every time there's a war. Popular during World War II and the Korean conflict. Hit its highest number of sales in 1966–67, during the Vietnam War.

A theory is only as good as its ability to predict behavior. Mendeleev predicted that the blanks in his periodic table would be filled with elements of certain atomic weights and properties. The subsequent discoveries of gallium, scandium, and germanium bore out his predictions. Einstein's special theory of relativity correctly predicted the deflection of light by the sun, tested out by the 1919 eclipse. Wegener's theory of continental drift was corroborated by fossils and satellite photographs. And Fleming's penicillin saved Winston Churchill's life during World War II.

The bellwether theory of chaotic systems is just that, and Ben and I are still in the early stages of our research. But I'm willing to hazard a few predictions:

HiTek will switch acronyms at least twice in the next year, establish a dress code, and make the staff hold hands and nurture their inner children.

Dr. Turnbull will spend all of next year attempting to handicap the Niebnitz Grant, to no avail. Science doesn't work like that.

I predict a number of new fads out of Prescott, Arizona, or Albuquerque or Fort Worth. Boulder, Seattle, and L.A. will fade out as trendsetters. Forehead brands will be big, and dental floss, and bobbed hair, particularly the marcel wave, will make a comeback.

As to the spiritual, angels are out and fairies will be in, particularly fairy godmothers, which, after all, do exist. Merchandisers will make a killing on them and then lose their shirts trying to anticipate the next craze.

I predict a sharp decline in sheep-raising, an increase in weddings, and no change at all in the personals. The hot dessert this fall will be pineapple upside-down cake.

And in some company or research institute or college, an overqualified mail clerk who is overweight or wears fur or carries a Bible will be hired, and the scientists therein would do well to remember their childhood fairy tales.

There will be a sharp upswing in significant scientific breakthroughs, and chaos, as usual, will reign. I predict great things.

This morning, I met Flip's replacement. I'd gone up to Stats to collect my hair-bobbing data, and she was coming out of the copy room, trailing someone's memos behind her.

She had lavender hair, arranged in a fountain effect, with several strands of barbed wire wrapped around it. She was wearing a bowling shirt, pedal pushers, black patent tap shoes, and orange lipstick.

"Are you the new mail clerk?"

She pursed her orange lips in disdain. "It's *workplace mes-*

sage facilitation director," she said, emphasizing every syllable. "And what business is it of yours, anyway?"

"Welcome to HiTek," I said, and would have shaken her hand except that she was wearing a barbed-wire ring.

Great things.

About the Author

CONNIE WILLIS has received six Nebula Awards and five Hugo Awards for her fiction, and the John W. Campbell Award for her first novel, *Lincoln's Dreams*. Her first short story collection, *Fire Watch*, was a *New York Times* Notable Book, and her latest novel, *Doomsday Book*, won the Nebula and Hugo Awards. She is also the author of *Impossible Things*, a short story collection, *Uncharted Territory*, and *Remake*. Ms. Willis lives in Greeley, Colorado, with her family.